The Unvisibles

Ian Whybrow

Holiday House / New York

Library of Congress Cataloging-in-Publication Data
Whybrow, Ian.
The Unvisibles / by Ian Whybrow.
p. cm.
Originally published: London : Macmillan, 2003.
Summary: After twelve-year-old Oliver recites an ancient Indian magical spell
and becomes invisible, he enlists the aid of his classmate, Nicky,
and the two of them join forces to undo the damage as well
as to help their families and themselves.
ISBN 0-8234-1972-X (hardcover)
[1. Magic—Fiction. 2. Friendship—Fiction. 3. England—Fiction.] I. Title.
PZ7.W6225Un 2005
[Fic]—dc22
2005040235

ISBN-13: 978-0-8234-1972-2
ISBN-10: 0-8234-1972-X

For my great friend, Dave Mander

Contents

Joining the Dots

It's early summer in the sunlit Art Room of Honnington House Secondary, a school for boys situated in a small seaside town in Kent called Marlbrook. Tinny music is ticking from Mr Tennyson's radio, to remind the class that Art is more fun than the other subjects. The class is having a go at pointillism. They have just learned about the pointillists, the French artists of the nineteenth century who created scenes by patiently applying thousands of dots of colour to canvas or board.

Two of the boys in particular are enjoying themselves, though in very different ways. Five minutes into the exercise and the tall one with the red hair and the sticky-out ears has already lost patience. This is Oliver Gasper. He is pounding his piece of sugar-paper, not with one felt-tip pen but with a fistful of them. He is hastily trying to cover up his scribbled creation, an Ultimate Level *Willybeast* attacking Mr Purvis, his French teacher. He is tremendously pleased by the brilliance of his specially invented computer-game character with its incredibly rude weapon-system. He is so delighted by the surprised look he has drawn on the teacher's face that his shoulders are shaking as he struggles to swallow whoops of hysterical laughter. Almost everybody in the room (including Mr Tennyson who has chosen to pretend not to) has seen the Willybeast and reacted in some way, mostly by shrugging or by flapping at it, as if it were an irritating mosquito. Some of the boys nearby have flicked paint and ink of their own on to it and its giggling creator. Chris Grover has tutted and told him to get a life. Oliver both admires and hates Chris Grover, who is the clever and brutal captain of every team going, so this remark has hit home painfully.

Meanwhile, in a much quieter way, Nicky Chew is also having a good time. He is the boy, one desk from the back, who has carefully dressed and groomed himself to be indistinguishable from any other ordinary kid of his age. There is nothing remarkable about the way he wears his uniform tie or about the length of shirt that hangs over his belt. True, the front of his normal hair is gelled just enough to allow it to be flicked up, but this has never attracted any comment. He is so caught up in his work that he is the one person in the room who is completely unaware of the stir that Oliver is creating. He is patiently dotting on his sheet of paper a small section of rippling water. The picture that the class is supposed to be copying is called *Bathers at Asnieres* by Georges Seurat. Nicky has chosen to use poster paint and three fine brushes of differing thickness. For some reason, the number three is important to him. He will seldom enter a room without squeezing the door handle three times, for example, or turning round three times. He has never asked himself why, but perhaps it has something to do with the fact that he worries quite a lot. Perhaps it makes him feel more confident about things when they're connected with a lucky number.

Nicky is interested to discover that water in a painting

doesn't have to be simply blue or green. He has used very little of either colour and is concentrating on blending dots of pink and white and grey. He is quite happy to go on quietly creating the rippling water and not to bother with the people sitting on the riverbank, gazing into the water at the bathers as in the original picture. He has noticed the factory at the top of Georges Seurat's painting, and the bridge, and the trees on the left hand side, and he is particularly taken by the kid in the sunhat standing in the water cupping his hands and calling to someone. Nicky carries on working quietly and methodically, doing three dots at a time. He wants nobody except Mr Tennyson to see his work and his main concern is that it should be neither highly praised nor singled out as poor work. He hates drawing attention to himself.

At this point in their lives, these two very different boys have taken pains to avoid each other. They live next door to each other and they're in the same class at school, but they have seldom even spoken to each other before. Yet only a few days after this Art lesson in constructing a new world out of dots, they are destined to become inseparable friends. They will have no choice in the matter because, without Nicky, Oliver will disappear once and for all and, without Oliver, Nicholas will also have to remain – in his own way – permanently invisible.

1. The Gaspers

'Go easy, Oliver! Oliver, can you hear me? Are you *listening* to me?'

'What d'you say, Dad?'

'I said, ARE YOU LISTENING TO ME!'

'Course I am. What's up?'

'I said, if you keep shoving the thing like that, you're gonna crush my knuckles on the door frame! Take it steady.'

It was the evening of the Thursday of the Art lesson. Oliver and his father were outside their antiques corner shop at 30, Shelley Avenue, trying to get a large piece of furniture (a Welsh dresser) into the back of a relatively small purple van. You could hear them all the way up Shelley Avenue, probably right up as far as the main road. Sometimes you could hear the springs of the van creaking like an old bed.

The pair was what you might call *noticeable*. There were things about them that always got people's attention. For one thing, they made a lot of noise and they made sudden, alarming gestures with their arms and heads. They both had long, bright red hair, so straight that much of it could have been painted on, falling like curtains on either side of their large ears. They had pale complexions and nice, big, white teeth that stuck out just enough to make some people notice that feature even before they noticed the red hair or the ears.

The dresser they were struggling with was over two hundred years old. It had a double cupboard at the bottom, separated by one real and two false drawers from the shelves at the top. It came out of the parlour of a splendid country house in Northamptonshire where it had once shown off blue-and-white china cups and plates and jugs, all worth a fortune these days, if you can find them. It was heavy, especially if you were crouching in the van, holding the bottom part, trying to stop the cupboard doors falling open and trying to avoid tripping over two blue apple boxes full of books and odds and ends that lay behind you. That is exactly what Oliver's dad was doing and that was why the sweat was running into his eyes. That is why he was shouting at his boy all the time, telling him, 'It'll go in − *just* − if we go steady, Oliver! STEADY!! What do they teach you in school, for crying out loud? You can't keep your mind on anything!'

The van was twelve and a half years old and it had

Specialists in Pine
George Gasper and Son
Antiques and Curiosities

painted on its sides. A bit of a shame really, because it laid them open to lots of jokes about the Gaspers being antique and curious. Pine furniture was their main business and, as a matter of fact, the Gaspers were better known for their curiosities than for their antiques. To tell the truth, they sold a fair amount of old tat.

6

Oliver Gasper was the 'and Son' part of *George Gasper and Son*. He was almost exactly the same age as the van, which was new on the day when Oliver was born. His dad had been so proud of his baby son and his van then that they made him cry and upset the midwife. They also made him shout, 'Thank you, God!' out loud, which woke up all the other babies on the ward and got him chucked out of the hospital. He didn't mind at all, because at last he had a son to share his interest in Charlton Athletic FC and maybe come into the business with him.

Just at this moment, however, at twenty-eight minutes past six o'clock on a Thursday evening in early summer, Mr Gasper had gone right off both son and van. There were a number of reasons for this:

1. Mr Gasper had to deliver the dresser to a genuine antiques dealer who lived thirty kilometres away, knowing that he, *Reginald Pugh, Period Furniture*, was an upper-class crook who had talked him into selling it for far less than it was worth, just because business was bad and he (Mr Gasper) needed the money badly. He was heavily in debt and he'd rather recklessly promised his difficult daughter Carrie a car for her twenty-first birthday, which was due in a couple of days. She had never really forgiven him for going ahead with 'and Son', so he felt that splashing out on her most important birthday might soften her up a bit.

2. He had dealt with Reginald Pugh before and knew

that he'd argue the toss and pretend that he never agreed to pay thirty pounds for delivery.

3. Mr Gasper's wife, Mrs Harriet Gasper, who had by far the strongest muscles in the family and normally helped with awkward deliveries, was packing, getting ready for a four-day trip to Ireland in search of furniture made of old pine.

4. Carrie Gasper (Oliver's fierce sister aged nearly twenty-one, aforementioned) was dyeing her hair black or putting a plaster on a septic piercing; either way, she wouldn't come out of the bathroom. That's why it was Oliver, who couldn't concentrate, rather than Mrs Harriet Gasper or Miss Carrie Gasper, who was up the shelf end of the Welsh dresser right now.

Oliver was supposed to be helping his dad by going steady and easy, but his mind was not on the job. He was practising doing his 'groundsman's face' to get Adam Carter going. Carter was the intense, eager boy who sat several desks further forward from him in school and put his hand up all the time. Oliver hated the school groundsman and loved making Carter squeal. Doing the 'groundsman's face' involved turning down the left side of his mouth at the same time as rolling up his right eyeball until the green iris had disappeared and only the white part and the disgusting veins were showing. Oliver could do the groundsman's voice, too; he was a brilliant mimic. 'Get off my grass, you idiot boys!' he said in his head, with just the right amount of northern whine.

His dad was shaking with the strain of manoeuvring the dresser past the two apple boxes full of books and odds and ends that he had bought as a job lot with the Welsh dresser. He was thinking, One sudden move and I'll get my knuckles smashed on the door frame and my head whacked by the roof. And my back's breaking because of this stupid poky little van that I can't afford to replace. I've got a flaming great tax bill to pay, the shop needs decorating inside and out, I owe my brother fifteen hundred quid, I've got to be up at the crack of dawn to go chasing after new stock and I wish I could get my son to keep his mind on the job for more than two seconds at a time.

Oliver's upturned eyeball, unused to the cruel and unusual strain being put on it, chose this moment to be struck by a stabbing pain. Oliver gave a brief scream and then he immediately started thinking about something else. His thoughts went something like this: Why do I have to have stupid red hair and stupid sticky-out ears and teeth and why do I have to have a name like Oliver Gasper? Why can't I have just a normal name like Harry O'Donovan or Alpesh Patel so that people will stop taking the mickey out of me? Why do I have to go to school tomorrow and do a French test? I'll get all the answers wrong and everybody'll laugh, specially Mr Purvis and Chris Grover. Maybe if I tell Dad I've got one of my bad headaches, he'll let me stay at home because Carrie'll be in the shop and she can look after me.

Naturally, with all this on his mind, he was not paying attention to his dad shouting, 'Are you listening to me, Oliver? Steady now, just hold it there!' Still, he was vaguely aware that his dad wanted him to do *something*. With difficulty, he twiddled himself right round until his backside was pressing against the end of the dresser. He took a deep breath and gave a mighty backward heave.

Pause.

Even though she was right at the back of the house next door, and she was listening to a concert on Radio 3, Mrs Chew was startled by the noise Oliver Gasper's dad made as the skin got torn off his knuckles and his head got crushed against the roof of his small van by an old Welsh dresser. Mrs Chew was just old enough to remember going to a circus with performing animal acts when she was on a camping trip in France as a child. For a moment her blood ran cold because she suddenly felt certain that she had just heard an elephant going mad and breaking out of its cage.

2. The Chews

They were quiet people, the Chews.

There wasn't a Mr Chew, only Nicky Chew and Nicky Chew's mum, Sally. She was single and she was very pretty, but for a long time she had practised not showing it. She made sure her clothes weren't downright unfashionable but there was nothing trendy about her. She wore a little bit of make-up, but not enough to emphasize her beautiful eyes or mouth. If she'd ever gone missing and the police had asked people who knew her to help them create a photofit picture of her, everybody (except maybe Mr Dudzinski at Number 28) would have found it very hard to describe what she looked like, how tall she was . . . even whether she wore glasses. So it wasn't surprising that Nicky liked to remain invisible; she was the person he got the idea from.

The Chews' house, 32, Shelley Avenue, Marlbrook, Kent, was a nice little detached Edwardian villa. Not that you could see much of the elegant brick and stonework. It was almost entirely cloaked in red Virginia creeper, clematis, wisteria, and climbing hydrangea, all mixed up together, and chosen partly to provide continuous colour throughout the growing season, but also to wrap the house round like a leafy security screen. The lawns and flowerbeds, front and back, were trim and carefully tended. The house had been bought for Sally by

Grandpa and Grandma Chew, anxious people with plenty of money and what they called 'standards'. They were ashamed that Sally had had her baby, Nicholas Charles Chew, without being married and when she was just eighteen. In their hearts they felt she deserved to be homeless and wandering the streets. However, they reasoned that they had no choice but to do something for her since she had no husband to fall back on – and they certainly didn't want her falling back on Nicky's father, a young man whom she agreed was not committed to her, and whom they thought 'casual and inconsiderate'. So they hid her away in what they thought to be the suitably faraway town of Marlbrook.

They chose Shelley Avenue because they thought it was in a 'civilized' neighbourhood. They thought it might attract people with 'standards' to whom it mattered to live in an *avenue* where there were blossoming trees on both sides of the road. They explored carefully, ruling out buying anything in the neighbouring *streets* – Barnes Street and Tennyson Street – where they were disgusted to observe that some people had knocked down their front walls and concreted over their gardens in order to park their cars. Others, they noticed, had huge motorboats with names like *Shark Attack* and *Bodacious Lady* jammed in their driveways. There were houses painted orange or with fake Cotswold stone stuck on the brickwork to make them look oldie-worldie. They were pleased to see none of these 'horrors' in Shelley Avenue: no caravans; nobody walking a bull terrier on a chain; nobody *common*. There was a shop next door, certainly, but it was a respectable antiques shop, obviously just 'done up' and quite tastefully, too. So they decided that Number 32 would be exactly right for Sally and her baby. Then they helped Sally get a responsible job in a local bank, opened an account to help with nursery school fees and after that, more or less left her alone. In twelve years, they had seldom visited, though they had spoken briefly now and then on the telephone.

Sally was determined to shake off the snobbery and guilt that haunted her, and to bring up her child free from both, but it wasn't easy. She was understandably nervous about attaching herself to anybody else who might be as unreliable as Nicky's father. In Nicky's early years, she coped by keeping herself to herself, doing her best to make up for Nicky's unexpected arrival by making things as perfect as possible for him. She worked hard at the bank and equally hard at home. She kept everything spotless, chose only the most beautiful, tasteful furnishings she could afford, and decorated every room to perfection. She heaped her protective love on Nicky, carefully paying attention to all his needs and following up his interests – in books, drawing and painting and music.

She didn't mean to be stand-offish, but she could only cope if things were ordered and tidy, so she was understandably troubled by the growing mess at Number 30. Their business had obviously been going from bad to worse over the years. The shop and the rambling, sprawling living quarters over and behind it were in urgent need of a coat of paint. Gasper and Son began gradually spilling 'antiques and curiosities' onto the pavement in front of the shop and into the neglected back garden. Eventually, the latter was more or less a dumping ground for a collection of crumbling, concrete garden ornaments, rusting iron benches, bird tables and mounds of pine furniture in need of stripping and sanding. Nothing was said, but Nicky could feel his mother's discomfort and annoyance with the Gaspers. He winced with her when he heard the whine of their electric sanders and the booming of their loud voices and he kept well clear of them all.

The older he became, the clearer it became to Sally that what was lacking in Nicky's life was a father. Her women friends thought it was a waste for such a nice woman to stay single, so they made a point of agreeing with her that, seeing how shy her boy was, maybe he could do with a little masculine influence in his life. For these reasons she began to search, quietly, for her ideal partner. There was nobody at the bank to fit the bill. She occasionally permitted herself a date with a customer, but somehow none of the men she met quite suited. They were never quite bright or steady enough, quite responsible enough, quite *considerate* enough to be absolutely perfect for her – and equally importantly – for her son.

3. Mr Dudzinski

Almost a year to the day that she was startled by Mr Gasper's elephant-cry of rage and pain, Sally Chew's hopes had been raised temporarily by the arrival in the neighbourhood of a freelance photographer, Stefan Dudzinski who moved into Number 28. He was an attractive young man, full of life, cheerful, polite, keen to be friendly. The only trouble was, it seemed to Sally, he wasn't exactly *reliable*.

It wasn't long before he invited her out to dinner and she accepted his invitation. Unfortunately, he arrived three-quarters of an hour late with oil on his hands and shirt, and when they got to the restaurant, it turned out to be full. He'd booked a table, but it was somewhere else he couldn't remember the name of. On their second date, at a blues evening at The Winter Gardens in the next town, he neglected to tell her until half an hour before they set off that his car was out of action. But never mind, he thought she might enjoy going on his motorbike. Her own car was being serviced, so she didn't have much choice. But given that she wasn't dressed for motorbikes and that she'd taken the unusual step of visiting a hairdresser for this special occasion, she wasn't too pleased to have to change into trousers and mess up her expensive hairdo by squashing it into a crash helmet.

As it turned out, the concert was great, and she secretly felt that clinging to him on the motorbike was one of the most exciting experiences she'd had in her life. Unfortunately she didn't let Stefan know this. A warning voice in her head stopped her. And in the cold light of the following day, remembering the breathtaking angle at which he took corners, especially coming home, she decided that maybe Stefan was a bit *too* thrilling for someone like her. After all, she reasoned, she was supposed to be mature, steady and responsible. Supposing they'd had an accident, what would have happened to Nicky? Besides, Stefan Dudzinski was two years younger than her. And he was – well, eccentric. He was nice, but he could obviously be laid back to the point of being inconsiderate. That was bad. *Inconsiderate* was what Nicky's father had been. And besides, Stefan had no experience of looking after children. No, he wouldn't do. All in all, she thought she had better stop seeing him before it became too difficult to make a clean break. She had better look for an older man, preferably someone who had brought up a child.

After the concert trip, she turned down every invitation he offered, not without heartache on both sides. He was very keen, and there was a lot about him she liked: he was good-looking, gentle, funny, bright, brilliant at fixing things – but for Nicky's sake she couldn't afford to make another big mistake. So she stopped seeing him.

Nicky was disappointed, but then he and his mum could never actually bring themselves to talk about her and Mr Dudzinski directly. In fact, Nicky admired pretty well everything about him but he felt he would be betraying his mum if he mentioned this. So he kept it a secret that he was knocked out by the growl of Mr Dudzinski's motorbike, a Honda VFR. Nicky had looked it up on the Internet and discovered that it was capable of 160 mph and that it went from nought to sixty in 3.8 seconds. He also admired the shine of Mr Dudzinski's leather gear, the magnificence of his crash helmet not to mention the fabulous car that spent a great deal of time being restored and repaired in Mr Dudzinski's garage.

The car was a six-seater, 1929 Lancia Lambda (the type with the long chassis). It was entirely original, right down to the fabric roof-lining and the wickerwork basket seats in front. It is true that Mr Dudzinski had rewired the little sidelights that sat on top of the front mudguards so that they operated as flashing indicators, but he pointed out that he used an original switch. Since it was of such a great age, the car often called on Mr Dudzinski to adjust its tappets and reset its timing, tasks which he performed with endless patience while whistling cleverly through his front teeth.

Nicky had never known any adult to try out so many brilliant ways of avoiding walking. Mr Dudzinski would often Rollerblade effortlessly to his studio in town, but he was equally at ease on a variety of skateboards, an old-fashioned butcher's bike and a motorized aluminium scooter. It was true what his mother said about Mr Dudzinski's nails being oily, about his limited range of tunes for whistling, and about his hair being like a bird's nest. Still, Nicky thought he had a nice way of smiling, and he once passed a delicious chicken risotto over the back fence for Nicky and his mother to try. So why his mother didn't want anything to do with Mr Dudzinski, Nicky wasn't really sure. Maybe the problem was a private thing, like kissing or something. More likely it was just because, like him, she was a worrier.

Anyway, at the time Oliver and his dad were loading their van, Sally Chew was home from the bank and busy by the open window in the kitchen preparing a wholesome organic meal of fish with three steamed vegetables, including local broccoli. Nicky, on the other hand, didn't hear Mr Gasper's mad-elephant impression. That was because he was in the drawing room, practising part of a rondo by Mozart on his baby grand piano at that particular moment.

That's the sort of kid he was.

4. Mind Matters

The thirty-kilometre van ride to Stourley from Marlbrook was a miserable one for Oliver Gasper. The way was green and pleasant, mostly. Sometimes the sea flicked blue between the houses. But it all slid by Oliver without his noticing. His father stared grimly ahead, scowling, occasionally sucking his wounded knuckles and feeling his head for cracks. Now and then he muttered that if Oliver didn't get his act together quick, he was going to cancel his magazines, stop all his pocket money and confiscate his telly and PC. And just to be especially annoying, he tuned in to Classic FM. Normally, when he wasn't upset, he liked listening to the Golden Oldies on Radio 2. He would sing along to them noisily, doing John Lennon and Tina Turner impressions. They were his best, though he was pretty good at Bob Dylan, Rod Stewart and Elvis Presley. Normally he encouraged Oliver to join him, grinning and slapping him on the back in time to the music, proud of the fact that his boy was just as good at doing voices as he was, maybe better.

Oliver was thinking about school tomorrow. His plan to avoid his humiliating Trial by French Test by pleading a headache was doomed. He knew that if he mentioned a pain anywhere, his still-fuming father would say, 'Good, serves you right'. And since he wasn't in the mood for admiring passing fields and hedgerows in a summery early-evening light, there was little for Oliver to do but pick his nose. He did so thoroughly, as if he were a sort of nasal Christopher Columbus, exploring the farthest, uncharted reaches of his nostrils for the first time, until his dad gave his shoulder a shove and told him to pack it in.

Oliver's experiment with a cassette that he found on the floor (to find out whether it was possible to push it into the tape-slot in the dashboard with his feet) almost killed the pair of them at the junction with the Canterbury Road. Once the squabble over that had died down, the only way that Oliver could think of for dealing with the remaining bad vibes and for passing the time, was to investigate one of the two apple boxes of books and odds and ends that were now squashed on to the seat between them. Mr Gasper had hoiked them out from under the Welsh dresser at the last moment to allow the whole thing to be laid flat on the floor at the back of the van.

Oliver was not what you might call a bookish boy. It is true that occasionally he found a use for books – like, for example, tapping Alex Holdroyd on the head with one when he was racing away with his Comprehension exercises. Then again, a large book, such as an atlas, when propped up on his desk served as a valuable screen from the prying eyes of Mr Tranter during Geography, while Oliver was resting his head for a minute or two, or picking lumps off his rubber to flick at Henry Wilton. But as reading material, books were a last resort.

So it was desperation that drove Oliver to rummage

among the dusty volumes in the top box beside him. Out came *The Wanderings of Odysseus*, *The Scarlet Letter* and Lamb's *Tales from Shakespeare*. None of them offered him any relief from his misery. *The Rubaiyat of Omar Khayyam*, translated from the French by Baron Corvo, had some uncut pages, even some bright illustrations but, essentially, nothing Oliver thought worth looking at.

He gave up on the top box to have a rummage in the one underneath, though the edge of the box dug painfully into his wrist. He managed to work his fingers under the top layer of books and magazines eventually. He felt plenty of china – including a jug, maybe, or a pot and some dishes – and he could feel the rough edges of frames and the grimy glass of a bunch of old photos or pictures, pressed upright together against the far side of the box. The shop was crammed full of such junk, which held no interest for him at all, so he let them lie without bothering to take them out and look at them. As he withdrew his aching arm he found that he had a reason-able grip on a magazine of some sort. With difficulty, he tugged it out from under the top box without ripping off too much of its cover, and looked it over. It was yellow-ing, crumpled, and its dry edges were beginning to disintegrate like burned flaky pastry but, surprisingly, its title *Mind Matters* was enough to catch his very-hard-to-grab attention. At least it was enough to make Oliver wonder idly, 'Why?' and to start flicking through its musty pages.

The flicking sent up a cloud of dust. In seconds, his dad was sneezing his head off. 'Flippin' 'eck, Oliver!' he roared. The engine screamed and the van snaked, as by turns his nose exploded and he wrestled with the steering wheel. Oliver braced himself between the door and the boxes with his elbows, and waited impatiently for the print to settle down so that he could read the next bit.

5. A Considerate Man

Nicky did the full twenty minutes practice on his Mozart, playing the same section three times – just to be on the safe side. He liked to please his mum and, like her, he hated any sort of fuss. But that wasn't the main reason. The truth was, he was doing the three-business more and more these days, fearing that if he didn't go through his little perfection-ritual, his mum would end up letting Robbie Williams get married to her.

This was not Robbie Williams the singer. This was a smarmy bloke with the same name, who only ever turned up in suits, mostly green ones. This Robbie Williams was one of a number of men (Nicky couldn't stand any of them) who had answered his mum's advertisement in the newspaper. When she showed it to Nicky and tried to explain how important this step was for both of them, he couldn't help noticing how tense she was, how much her hand was trembling. So what could he do, except to give the words she had written a smile and nod of support?

Bright and capable single mother (29) with wonderful son (12) seeks close relationship with considerate, sensitive, single father, possibly leading to marriage. The relationship must also bring joy and balance to son's life.

But as far as Nicky was concerned, he'd got plenty of joy and balance in his life already. His mum was beautiful and kind and his best friend, so they were comfortable together. Personally, he couldn't think what was wrong with Mr Dudzinski if she *had* to get married, but if she didn't want him, why couldn't they just be ordinary and quiet and not have to live with an over-dressed person with a trick name and a false laugh, who smelled like a stale face flannel? Not that he could bring himself to tell her, of course.

Third time round on the same section of the Mozart, Nicky hit the notes extra loud to drown out the memory of the fact that (the fake) Robbie Williams had dated his mum six or seven times now and that she had told Nicky, 'I think he's a very nice man, very thoughtful, very considerate. What do you think, Nicky?'

'Considerate' was one of Sally Chew's top ten words. In fact, it was probably in her top three.

Things were getting dangerous.

6. Focusing

Bouncing Oliver Gasper (the road got very bad after Brockbridge) found that he was unexpectedly engrossed in an article in *Mind Matters* entitled 'The Indian Rope Trick – An Investigation into the Ancient Art of Vanishing'. Where had he heard of the rope trick before? Seen it in a comic somewhere, maybe? As he read on, a vivid picture sprang into his mind of an almost naked Indian man in a turban sitting cross-legged and playing a funny looking pipe in front of a small basket. Instead of a cobra popping up and starting to sway, a rope uncoiled itself. It rose straight up into the air and balanced like a pole, without any visible means of support. The climax of the trick came when the man put down his pipe and shimmied up the rope. And when he got to the top – he vanished.

Normally, Oliver wouldn't have had the staying power to struggle with the long words, especially when the movement of the van made them specially hard to read. But the thought of being able to vanish appealed strongly to him, what with the French test coming up. And the detention. A terrible heat rose in Oliver as he remembered yesterday's humiliation when the gentle Mr Tennyson had finally lost patience with the Willymon business and stuck him in detention. It was the first DT Mr Tennyson had ever given, so he said. His dad would go ballistic if he found out, and now the class had another excuse to keep panting out his name, taking the mick – '*Gaspah-ah-ah-ah-ah-ah!*'

Oliver imagined himself halfway up a rope that sprouted from his desk like a beanstalk, calling, 'So long, everybody!' and waving bye-bye to a gob-smacked Mr Purvis who had just asked the class to write down the third person singular form of the present and imperfect tenses of the verbs *connaitre, faire* and *pouvoir*. How brilliant to get away from all that, to be able to escape his sarcastic remarks about Gasper the Exasperator. How soothing to rise above the sneers of the whole crowd of mickey-takers, especially that clever bighead and hard man, Chris Grover. '*Gaspah-ah-ah-ah-ah-ah!*' His skin and scalp prickled with a panicky sweat. No way was he going in to school tomorrow.

His dad, sensing that something was wrong, took his eyes off the road for a second and was surprised to see his usually twitchy, fidgeting, irritating son applying himself quietly and with intense, almost fierce, concentration to the jumping yellow pages of some old magazine.

'What you got there, son, Page Three?' he laughed, happy to be cheery again, trying to be man-to-man.

Oliver didn't hear him. He ploughed on with his reading. *The disappearance of such a performer,* wrote a Professor Svartvik, *was often till now considered to be a matter of raising certain expectations in the minds of the assembled spectators. It was, if you will, a matter of mass hypnosis.* Oliver wasn't sure he got that, but he kept going. *However, there is some evidence that there are certain remarkable individuals who can so concentrate their own minds that they are able, by a supreme effort of will, to transport themselves physically into a different state of being.* That bit was straightforward enough. *One such master,* went on the professor, *a holy man of Gujarat, confided to me that he often achieved this exalted state simply by focusing his mind upon a single phrase, one which he chanted inwardly, never ceasing until he had done so thirty-three times and three again and three again, that number being both sacred and auspicious . . .*

'What's "au . . . auspic . . ."?' Oliver asked out loud, stammering with the effort. And then, before his dad could answer, 'Looks a bit like "suspicious" only with an "au" at the front.'

'Haven't got a clue, son,' said his dad. 'Why?'

But Oliver was lost in the article again. He had already decided that 'auspicious' probably meant 'lucky' or 'good'. He wasn't stupid, not when he put his mind to something. Now he was looking at the words the holy man said thirty-three times plus three plus three to make himself vanish. Translated, according to the professor, they meant something like, 'I am elsewhere suddenly'.

All you had to do was empty your head of everything else, get focused, say *I am elsewhere suddenly* in your head thirty-three times plus three plus three, and you could step into another state of being. And if you wanted to come back, all you had to do was 'reverse the phrase'. Wouldn't that be fantastic!

He stared hard at the words: *Chhoo muntar jaldi.*

Did 'reverse the phrase' mean you had to say the words in reverse order – *jaldi muntar chhoo*? Or did it mean you had to say the words backwards? Oliver was so pre-occupied by trying both – *jaldi muntar chhoo* and *idlaj*

27

ratnum oohhc – that he didn't register that the van had arrived at a small, neat village with a proper village green where black-and-white, half-timbered houses leaned at funny angles to show how old and English they were. It was only when the van bumped up the kerb on to some flagstones in front of an imposing bay window that threw the dazzling reflection of the low sun into his eyes, that he twigged that they'd reached Stourley. In fact, they had reached their destination, the shop belonging to Reginald Pugh, Period Furniture.

Hastily Oliver plucked the biro from behind his dad's ear and scribbled *Chhoo muntar jaldi* on the back of his hand.

'Hoy, you cheeky so-and-so . . . !' yelled his dad. 'What's got into you today, Oliver? Give us that back!' He snatched the pen and replaced it behind his other ear. He also snatched the magazine and stuffed it into the box among the other odds and ends.

7. Robbie and Riley

Nicky said no thanks, not more broccoli, though he actually liked broccoli. His mum replaced the delicate lid of the steaming porcelain serving dish and moved the vase of Dutch irises slightly to her left, so that she could see her son more clearly across the table.

'. . . and he's been married before,' she said carefully. 'And he has one child, a little boy. He's nine. And we share a lot of interests, what with him working in finance too . . .'

Nicky kept chewing, though he didn't need to. Three chews, then three more lots of three.

'And I know you'll get to like him, Nicky, once you've met him a few more times, because he's really keen on all sorts of things I'm hopeless at. Like . . . you know . . . names of aeroplanes, orienteering, that sort of thing. Birdwatching, he's keen on. Birding, they call it. And he's an expert on light opera. But he loves sports. Not that he's one of those beer-swilling, down-the-pub types. No, he likes rugger . . .'

'We play football at school,' said Nicky, just by the way.

'Yes, well, he'll know all about that. He's very rounded. He's good at – you know – taking people out of themselves, do you know what I mean? I mean, I worry about you, Nicky, just having me around all the time, and not having enough, well, man-to-man talk. And he's very . . .'

'Considerate . . .' added Nicky.

'Anyway, he's coming over tomorrow for supper. And he's bringing Riley to meet you.'

'Riley?'

'Unusual, isn't it? That's the name of his little boy. He's very musical too, apparently, sings all the time, wants to be an opera singer when he grows up. I haven't met him yet, but I'm sure he'll be good fun and you'll both get on like a house on fire. And they're coming over tomorrow evening – this'll make you smile. They're going to "make us a proposition" – both of us.'

Nicky managed a weak smile.

'Because Robbie wants us all to be part of this – not just him and me. And I thought that sounded very sensible, don't you?'

'Is there any more turbot, Mum?' said Nicky, meaning, *I don't want to be selfish, Mum, but I don't think I feel ready for Robbie and Riley and I don't want bringing out of myself. Anyway, 'proposition' sounds scarily like 'proposal'.*

Sally Chew reached towards the fish dish. There was plenty more fish. She thought Nicky really wanted more fish. 'So that suits you, does it, love?'

Nicky was thinking, *Please, God, No* times three and his mum was thinking how marvellous it was that her little boy was taking such a grown-up view of things by agreeing with her. But she was interrupted, not to say shaken, by a shriek of agony from the kitchen of Number 28, followed by a shockingly inventive stream of curses.

Nicky ran out into his garden and stood by the fence. The only way to get a clear view of what was happening on the other side of it was to stand on top of the rockery. This was not the sort of thing Nicky would normally have done, especially as he was not supposed to be on speaking terms with Mr Dudzinski. On the other hand, this sounded like an emergency. Treading carefully so as to avoid the tender alpine plants, he picked his way to the top of the rockery and peered over the fence into the wilderness of Mr Dudzinski's garden.

'Careful, Nicky,' said his mum, unnecessarily.

'Oo! Ah! Oo!' said Mr Dudzinski, hearing voices and moderating his language.

'What's happening? What's the matter with Mr Dudzinski?' said his mum.

Nicky did his best to do justice to the scene that met his eyes. Thick black smoke was pouring from his open kitchen door and Mr Dudzinski himself was tearing round in the long grass, alternately waving his hands in the air like a gospel singer and tucking them under his armpits.

'Won't be a tick, Mum,' said Nicky, and scrambled over the fence to help. He checked that there was no fire in the kitchen before opening all the windows to air the house then fetched Mr Dudzinski a coat to put round him for the shock. It took a little time after that to piece together what had happened, but he managed eventually. Mr Dudzinski had left four slices of Welsh rarebit to toast under the grill of his top oven. They had carried on toasting while he returned to his garage to double-check the fibre coupling transmission (it connects the prop-shaft to the gear shaft and back axle, he explained to Nicky, guessing correctly that he was interested to know that sort of thing). The cheese had then done what very hot cheese does, and caught fire. So had the rubber seal round the door of the oven, which sent thousands of little soot particles into the air that descended leaving oily smears on paintwork, cupboards, worktops and floor – wherever they landed. Mr Dudzinski had risen to the occasion by flinging a wet tea towel at the blaze, but in lifting the grill pan and running with it into his garden, he had chargrilled the tips of his fingers to a crisp turn.

The last thing Nicky expected was that his mother should leap over the fence and administer first aid and sympathy. But that was what she did, clucking and wincing with him when things got too painful. And though all his fingers were bandaged and tender, he was persuaded to come round and share their warmed-up supper. He even managed, with a little spoon-feeding from Sally, to finish off the turbot, broccoli, green beans and Jerusalem artichokes that remained on the Chews' table. He said they were delicious and apologized for getting so much of the creamy sauce down his shirt. He was invited to leave it to be washed, and since he couldn't easily manage the buttons, his mum had to give him a little help with those too. Then she – with Nicky, of course – went with him to Number 28 to inspect the oven and the smoke damage. She pronounced the oven to be beyond repair, advised on its replacement, suggested a good painter and decorator and made one or two practical enquiries. Would it be helpful, for example, if Nicky assisted Mr Dudzinski ('Please call me

Stefan – or Dud if you like') into his pyjamas. No need, he didn't wear pyjamas. Oh. Really? Well that was all right, then.

Later, Nicky asked his mum how come she'd invited him to eat if she wasn't talking to him.

'Well, it would only have gone to waste,' was her practical reply.

8. The Rip-off

Oliver's dad didn't have time to get too worked up by the pen-snatching business because Major Reginald Pugh (retired) himself had appeared, an irritated look lifting the bushy eyebrows high on his broad, pink face. He had one of those heads of hair that a lot of rich, self-important men have. It was dark, thick, oily and scraped back on both sides of a not-quite central parting. He looked down his narrow, superior nose as he flipped his pocket watch out of his check waistcoat by its gold chain and slapped it into his palm. 'What kept you chaps?' he said. 'Did you come via Herne Bay or something?'

'Got here as soon as we could,' muttered Mr Gasper, smiling back. Oliver was sad to observe how his dad let this man put him down, but he also knew how hard up he was. This sale was important.

The Major didn't move a muscle to help get the dresser out of the van. He let Oliver and his dad, knees sagging, backs straining, do all the work, making a big thing out of holding the door of his shop open and flicking specks of something unwelcome off the lapels of his double-breasted blazer and his regimental tie. When they were inside, he let them get on with it while he stepped over to the expensive laptop that hummed and flickered on his desk, typed a few words and closed a document.

'There! Another email wings its way. Another

satisfied customer of www.periofurn.co.uk. Must keep up with the times, give the customers what they want, eh, don't you think? I gather you Gaspers haven't got a website yet! You really should, you know, George. Put the dresser down next to that chest of drawers. Mind that long-case clock, for God's sake!'

'Handsome, isn't it?' said Mr Gasper, meaning the dresser, straightening himself slowly and giving his back a rub. 'Come from the Darnley House sale, up Northampton way. Lovely colour, eh? Fruitwood this is, unusual. Nice moulded cornice, look. Pierced frieze round the top of the plate rack, smashin'! And no sign of worm – just a bit of wetting round her feet where they mopped the stone floor. Adds value, that. And it's got all the original hooks and door furniture, of course. Should get you two and a half grand, no problem.'

'Ah, but the shelves should *never* be screwed and glued to the base like that,' tutted Major Pugh.

'I know that, Reggie, but . . .'

'I'm sticking at eight hundred and fifty pounds, that's what we agreed. Cash, of course.' The Major started flicking fifty-pound notes off a wad.

George Gasper twitched a bit and ran his sore fingers through his hair. 'That only leaves me a hundred quid for a two-day job,' he sighed. 'And all that driving. Which reminds me. Don't forget you owe me thirty pounds for delivery.'

'Oh, come on, George! You never mentioned delivery charges,' smiled Reginald Pugh, shaking his head in a show of disbelief at the cunning and sheer *greed* of this suggestion.

'You know flippin' well I did. We agreed thirty quid!' Oliver's dad was ready for that one. He worked his thumbs under his waistband and hoiked up his trousers to show he meant business.

'All right, all right, no need to raise your voice. We're all friends here, aren't we?' The Major slowly peeled off three tenners. 'Did you pick up anything else from Darnley House?' he went on, casually. 'Missed the sale myself. I was over in France for a few days, actually. Ever go there? I've got a place there, converted farmhouse. Lovely. I'm there all the time, love it. As a matter of fact, I'm popping over again this weekend. Any excuse to give the old Jag a bit of a spin, as you can imagine!'

'Smashing car,' said Mr Gasper, avoiding Oliver's look because they both knew what a fat chance there was of them affording anything like that.

'Anyway,' the Major drawled on, 'I saw the Darnley House sale catalogue, naturally. Apparently the family used to be rolling in money and the house was full of very interesting pieces. I gather that Great-Grandpapa Darnley spent a good deal of his youth in Paris in the 1880s and 1890s, lucky fellow. He knew all the Impressionists, you know, including the pointillists. Bought quite a lot of paintings for a song at one stage, they say, but they all got sold in the 1930s to pay off debts . . . Familiar story, eh? Such a pity – because they'd be worth a *fortune* these days!' He noticed Oliver squirming with irritation and boredom. 'Of course, you'd know all about the Impressionists, wouldn't you, laddy?' he said, giving Oliver's ear a tug.

'Course I do!' blurted Oliver, furious that Major

Pugh had touched him on a sensitive part. 'We done them in Art.'

'Ah, you *done* the Impressionists, did you? Name me some!'

Oliver was embarrassed by his grammatical 'mistake' now. He'd said it deliberately to annoy Major Pugh; now Reginald had turned it against him. How he wished he'd listened harder in Art. 'Well, there was Renoir for one,' he said. 'And . . .'

'Come on, Oliver, you tell Major Pugh,' pleaded his dad, longing for the boy to show this smug, self-satisfied, upper-class creep a thing or two.

'The bloke who did all the dots,' Oliver blurted.

'Ah, the pointillists! Now could that be Sisley? Monet? Pissaro? Come along, come along, final answer? Have to hurry you . . . Would you like to phone a friend? Ha, ha!'

Oliver's mind went blank. He'd let himself down, and his dad.

'Dear, oh dear, education today, eh?' said Reginald Pugh. 'Honestly, George, where did it all go wrong? Kids get away with murder, fiddling about, wasting time. Pity they won't bring back the stick, eh? Thrash a few facts into them, make them sit up and take notice, I say! Don't you agree, old boy?'

'Well, I couldn't really name two Impressionists either, could I, Oliver?' answered Mr Gasper. He shifted towards his son. It was only a little movement, but it was enough to show he felt for the boy and wanted to support him. Oliver was so touched that his eyes brimmed with tears. He was furious with himself and had to turn aside to blink them away. 'I'm flippin' hopeless on painters,' his dad went on. 'Furniture's more my thing. I'd like to have had some of that art nouveau stuff they had in the sale, but that was a bit too pricey for me. No, I picked up this old dresser and a couple of boxes of odds and ends, that's all. Few books, few knick-knacks, that was my lot. Haven't had time to take a proper look at 'em. Still got to sort 'em out. Never mind, I know there's one book might be worth a few quid for the prints alone. *Omar Khayyam* or something. Translated by some baron. Lovely condition. Even got a dust jacket.'

Reginald Pugh's piggy eyes took on a greedy shine. The book sounded as if it might just be a 1924 edition of *The Rubaiyat of Omar Khayyam*, translated from the French by Baron Corvo. A rarity indeed! 'All right, all right, I'll do you a favour. Take it off your hands for you for fifty pounds – sight unseen, what do you say? I trust your judgement, George, you see – and I know you've been having a bit of a cash-flow problem lately. But listen, you don't want to waste your time fooling around with pine furniture. No money in it, except the really old stuff and the Yanks grab that. People don't want it, old boy! They want the Real Stuff these days. Proper antiques is the name of the game, not tarted-up junk.'

Mr Gasper's pale face took on a beaten spaniel look that made Oliver want to smack Reginald Pugh's head in. So what if his dad did sell junk? His dad was an expert furniture restorer. And what's more, *he* didn't rip people off.

'Can we go, Dad?' he mumbled.

'. . . thirty, forty, fifty crisp ones . . . there. And I'll take *The Rubaiyat* off your hands,' said Reginald Pugh.

Mr Gasper accepted the money with a resigned nod. 'All right, son,' he said. 'Let's just have a pee and then we'll push off home.'

'I'll pick up the book while you pop out the back,' said Pugh. 'It's in a box, you say?'

'Yeah, there's a couple of boxes on the front seat. It's in the top one,' Mr Gasper called after him.

It was only when they were nearly home, after a journey where neither the boy nor his dad could find anything much to say to each other, that they noticed. They were both musing on the humiliating way Reggie Pugh had treated them; and they'd had to let him! So they had travelled twenty-odd kilometres before they registered the fact that both the boxes were missing from the front seat of the van.

'The crafty so and so!' breathed Mr Gasper. 'He's only gone and nicked the lot!'

'He was only supposed to take that book, wasn't he?' said Oliver. 'D'you want to go back and fetch back the other stuff? That could be worth a fair bit. Go on, I don't mind, honest, Dad.'

'Nah, it's good of you, son . . . but I doubt it. I only paid a few quid for both boxes. Anyway, you know what he's like. He'll only say, "*But, George, old boy, you said it was thirty crisp ones for the lot!*" '

'Yeah, but I'm a witness, Dad!'

'Nah, I don't s'pose there was anything worth having, only the one book,' yawned Mr Gasper. 'Bit of china, few pictures – all rubbish. The auctioneers always check everything over loads of times. They would have sorted out anything really valuable.'

'Well they missed the book, didn't they?' said Oliver.

'Just a fluke,' said his dad, letting go of the steering wheel for a second to scratch under both arms at once. 'Come on, son, I'm tired, I've got a long journey tomorrow and you've got school. We need our beauty sleep. Let's call it a day.'

Let's call it a nightmare, thought Oliver. And I still can't remember the name of that bloke that did dot paintings, that one Mr Tennyson was talking about yesterday. God, I'm so thick. He glanced down at his hand and saw the words *Chhoo muntar jaldi*. Repeating it thirty-three times plus three plus three would do the trick, eh? Not that many, really. It was the 'focusing' bit that was tough. Suddenly it came to him. *Seurat! Monsieur Sewer-rat! That was the name of that pointillist bloke!* Encouraged by this, he had a little go at repeating *Chhoo muntar jaldi*, but every time he'd said it four times over in his head, other things started sneaking in. Like the fact that he was starving hungry.

Like the beaten, disappointed look on his dad's face.

Like the image of the greedy snout of Major Reginald Pugh rooting among the stuff in the boxes he'd stolen.

9. An Awakening

Christopher Grover had Oliver Gasper in a choking neck lock. He was wrestling him towards the edge of a cliff in a howling gale whilst Mr Purvis, silk tie flapping over his shoulder, bent over them, clapping his hands and shouting encouragement: '*Très bien*, Monsieur Grover! The last gasp for Monsieur Gasper, *n'est-ce pas? Encore, s'il vous plait! Répétez!*'

Oliver felt Grover's knees in his back then his feet between his shoulder blades. Suddenly he was cannoned into space, twisting like a wind-blown newspaper. As he tumbled, screaming, it rushed through his mind that he must try to wake up before he got smashed to pieces on the rocks below. Otherwise he would die of a heart attack. That was the rule of dreams.

Luckily, it was the screaming that saved Oliver; not his own, but his dad's and his big sister's. They were having a good, loud go at each other, as they often did these days, shouting and swearing their heads off.

'It's not much to ask you to get your lazy great carcass out of bed and put the kettle on and sort out your brother's something breakfast while your mother and I are trying to get on the something road!'

'Why can't he get his own something breakfast? I'll be stuck in that something shop all day! Let him make his own something toast!' yelled Carrie.

41

'Don't swear, and listen to what I'm telling you!' Mum was sticking her oar in now. 'You're to get him up, make sure he gets a proper breakfast and make sure he gets off to school. He was moaning about headaches last night, but he's only trying to skive off school. Your father and me are not having him sitting at home all day watching the something telly while we're flogging ourselves to death trying to save the business!'

'And we shan't be paying out for you to go driving about in some fancy little car if you don't stop coming the old acid and pull *your* something weight, my girl!' put in Dad.

'You *promised* me a car for my twenty-first, so don't start threatening, and don't you "my girl" me, you chauvinist pig!'

'Who are you calling a pig?'

Etcetera, etcetera.

When finally Oliver did summon up the courage to creep downstairs and into the kitchen, Mum and Dad had hit the road for Ireland, and the fumes of overdone toast and fry made his eyes water. Wisely, he accepted a plate of something charred without comment. He ate it all, too, as cheerfully as he could, though it had the texture of cat litter and probably the taste. He had to. His sister glared murderously at his image, which was reflected in the mirror she had propped on the microwave. She was daring him to complain while she twisted in seventeen of her piercings and (eventually) rubbed baby oil into her most recent and sorest tattoo.

When he had forced down the last of her burned offerings, she told him quietly that if he didn't wash up very nicely and then go to school, she would kill him. He believed her and he thought it was unkind and unnecessary of her to go on, 'Because I want that car, Oliver. And I do not want you giving Dad any something excuses for not getting it for me. Do you hear what I'm something well saying to you, Oliver?'

He did something well hear her and he believed her. That is why he made sure that he showed himself to her in his something school uniform (though he didn't let her see that he was wearing his trainers, rather than his black, regulation shoes). Then he made a big thing out of collecting up his schoolbooks and stuffing them into his bag. He also made sure that he slammed the something front door good and hard in an 'I'm off to school now' way.

Then he ducked out of sight behind the hedge before dashing commando-style down the side passage and taking cover in the welcome gloom of the shed in the back garden.

He settled down on the slippery plastic of a Gro-bag that was leaning against the shed wall, panicking nests of earwigs and centipedes as he squashed its damp contents to match the contours of his bottom. He disturbed a clutch of garden tools but grabbed them before they began to clatter. As the silence washed over him, he surrendered to his worries. He worried about French. He worried about everybody thinking he was an idiot. He worried about his dad carrying out his threat and taking all his comforts away. He worried about his mum and dad going broke. He worried that Carrie might creep up on him and drag him out of his hidey-hole by his hair. 'God, what a mess,' he breathed into his hands.

Suddenly, he heard people calling, quite close. He sat up so quickly that he whacked his head on a low shelf, sending plastic flowerpots cascading over him. He clutched wildly at them, desperately trying to smother the clatter. He held his breath and strained his ears till they whistled. Then came the voices.

'Oh, not too bad. We've got a French test, but nothing to worry about. It'll just be normal.' It was Nicky Chew. He was obviously just over the fence in next-door's back garden, calling out to his mum; he didn't seem to have noticed any unusual clattering.

'And you've got your sandwiches? Oh, and your celery sticks – I put them in the box with that dip you like – and did you put in that mango yogurt I got for you?' Mrs Chew's voice must be coming from their kitchen.

'Yes, Mum . . . honestly. I'm only going to school. I'm not going into the jungle, you know.'

'Sorry, love. I'm just a bit tense. It's our big meeting with You-Know-Who and his little boy tonight, remember? So you will try to get home nice and early to give me a hand, won't you? I want everything to be just—'

'Don't worry, Mum, I haven't forgotten. I'll be here.'

'Well, give me a kiss and have a lovely day.'

Until this moment, Oliver had never given his neighbour much thought. Nicholas Chew was just a kid in his class, always getting on quietly with his work, always coping, apparently never bothered by anything, just boring really. Now, all of a sudden, Oliver couldn't help feeling rather jealous of him. '. . . We've got a French test, but nothing to worry about,' he'd said. And he had somebody bothering to make lunch for him? He even got a kiss goodbye.

Misery welled up in Oliver as it dawned on him that Nicky Chew had pretty well everything going for him because he was – well – *normal*. His hair was just normal-coloured, not a horrible ginger, and it did what hair is supposed to do without making a big thing of it. Nicholas's ears just sat there quietly on the sides of his head, folded back pleasantly, not asking at all to be compared to an Audi TT with the doors open, like his own. It was difficult to remember what colour Nicholas's eyes were because they were always turned away or down to his work. They were probably just a nice normal blue. Not little peepy green ones like mine, thought Oliver. As for his teeth, Nicholas's were exactly the sort that Oliver was going to get one day. One day, when he was rich and there was a law against drills, he was going to get the dentist to do genetic modification on his teeth. He was going to have them all made smaller and more or less the same size, so the front ones would just stay neatly behind his lips when he closed his mouth, like Nicholas's.

Nicholas was neither very tall nor very short and he wore neat, clean clothes that were more or less like everybody else's only maybe a bit less creased. He wasn't brilliant, not like Carter, nor a big hunky all-rounder like Grover. Mr Purvis never picked on him, never even spoke to him. Still, come to think of it, when a teacher, a nice one, say, like Mr Boardman, did bother to ask him something directly, Nicholas nearly always came up with the answer. He knew things. He knew which word had all the vowels in the correct order – 'facetious'. He knew ambergris came from whales. 'Like Mr Purvis, sir!' Oliver had shouted. 'He comes from Wales!' That was a good one that, brilliant, but not one person in the class even smiled at it. They hated him, that's why. Not one of them would let him copy their French.

'Everybody hates me. They all think I'm stupid. And everything's going wrong,' Oliver concluded. 'I'm just going to sit here in the dark all day.'

After a long time, he heard the snap of the lock on the back door of his house and the whirring of the awning as it was lowered. That meant that Carrie was on her way out front to open up the shop. About time. It must be well past nine by now.

He raised his wrist so that a shaft of light penetrating the cracks between two panels in the shed wall could light up his watch. The face of the watch showed up brightly. So did the writing on his unwashed hand.

Chhoo muntar jaldi

Oliver breathed in deeply and tried to breath out all his sadness, all the mess. He closed his eyes and tried to concentrate on the Indian rope trick. He began to whisper the words:

Chhoo muntar jaldi
Chhoo muntar jaldi
Chhoo muntar jaldi

Then he thought an earwig was crawling up his trousers. Startled, he brushed at his leg, drew in his breath and started again. This time he concentrated as if his life depended on it. Because, in a way, it did.

10. French Unseen

Period 5. French for 7R3. Mr Purvis was showing off, as usual. Luckily, since it wasn't far off lunch time, he couldn't muster the energy for a truly show-stoppingly cringe-making performance. He contented himself, as he made his sweeping entrance, with a short mouthful of flamboyant French that he obviously thought was clever enough to make a Frenchman faint with amazement, never mind a bunch of hopeless ignoramuses like 7R3. When he got to the '*Asseyez-vous*' bit, he flapped his hands up and down to signal to the really sad ones that they should now seat themselves. Then he went into his usual routine, pointing at the distant horizon and bopping various good-natured boys on the tops of their heads with a book when they felt sorry for him and looked where he pointed.

'*Eh bien, la classe, je vais vous mettre à l'épreuve*, meaning what? . . . Come on, come on!'

Villeneuve had Belgian parents and told him, 'You're going to test us, sir.'

'I'm surprised Gasper didn't have the answer to that one, eh Gasper? Where is my old Exasperator, *ce matin*?'

'He's absent, sir,' said Chapman.

Mr Purvis pulled out a large hanky, slapped the other hand on his bald head and pretended to sob. 'Oh no!

What a terrible shame! He's missed my special test with its gorgeous little Unseen Translation at the end!'

A groan from the class. He hadn't mentioned an Unseen before. 'Silence, you dogs!' he cried, cracking a pretend whip and shouting, 'Back! Get back!'

As a result of the polite laughter in response to that one, no one heard the door creak open – just a few centimetres – behind him. Perhaps it was the wind.

Mr Purvis resumed. 'If Gasper thinks he's got away with it, he's got another think coming. He'll have to do the test after school on Monday.'

The door opened wider. Eyes turned towards it, so that Mr Purvis noticed. He paused in his performance, and turned himself to see who it was. Nobody.

On with the show. 'Such a shame the Gasper's not here. I bet I know what he'd say if I asked him the French for "Shut the door". What would he say, Chris my old Grover of Academe?'

'Knowing how thick Gasper is, sir, he'd probably say, *Je ta door!*'

'Exactly! *Je t'adore!* Well done, Chris!'

Chris Grover waved his hands in front of his chest, snapping his fingers together gangsta rap style to show how cool he was.

The door banged sharply and made everyone jump.

'There you go, the door's Je t'itself!' giggled Mr Purvis. 'Shut itself, Stapleton, you thicko! *Je t'adore*, shut the door; Je t'it yourself, shut it yourself, come on, wake up at the back there!'

Then, quick as the flick of a chameleon's eyes, down came his serious face. It was time for Mr Purvis the

Serious Oxford Scholar. 'Papers out, Warburg!' he barked, slapping them down on Warburg's desk at the front. Warburg dashed up and down the aisles giving out test sheets while the teacher sank comfortably into his chair.

A silence fell, broken only by the scratch and tap of ballpoint pens and the occasional stifled yawn from the great man himself. He opened his book, a cricketing autobiography. He straightened his tie, which was decorated with cricket bats and balls, and began to identify with the brilliant thug whose meaty face grinned at the class from the cover of his paperback.

Nicky wasn't bothered about the length of the test. It was mostly fill-in-the-gap stuff, with just a few lines of 'unseen' translation at the end. He had mastered the present tense of every irregular verb known to 7R3 and more. He wasn't put off by the fact that Mr Purvis had slipped in one or two tricky agreements between nouns and adjectives. And the short Unseen − a translation from French into English at the end − was a doddle. Even so, he didn't rush to earn a hundred per cent; that would put him in the limelight. Instead, he took his time choosing which three he would get wrong. Always three for safety. And always best to keep a low profile.

As lunch came creeping up from the canteen with fried onions on its breath, Nicky caught a warm blast of something sweeter. A real warm blast, it was, just as if somebody was breathing directly into his ear. 'Juicy Fruit,' he thought vaguely and, a second later, somebody whispered, 'Listen, you've got to help me!'

It was so unexpected that he gave a little cry and

jerked his head. Everybody turned towards him. Mr Purvis looked up from his book. He said nothing, only raised his brow, placed his finger on his lips and resumed his reading.

Nicky was shaken. He hated attention. He side-spied up at his neighbour, Aziz. He couldn't for the life of him think how Aziz had managed to lean close enough to whisper right in his ear without being seen. But years of self-discipline closed in on him like the waters of the sea and he settled once more to his task.

He hadn't got much further than agreeing *blanches* with *maisons* when the Juicy Fruit smell overpowered the fried onion again. Just to be on the safe side, he placed his left forefinger in his ear, pretending he was having a scratch. As he did so, he felt as though someone had taken hold of his pen hand! It was as if somebody was squeezing his fingers tighter round the neck of his Pentel Rollerball and guiding it rapidly across the page. Nicky watched in astonishment as his hand moved, first in an arc, then a loop, then a sweep. Something shocking was happening on his test paper. With a rising sense of panic, Nicky found himself drawing some strange creature he didn't recognize.

'It's a Willybeast. Great, innit?' Again the Juicy Fruit voice.

Nicky wanted to protest, to shout, but he felt as if an arm had reached across his chest and an elbow was digging into his shoulder, pressing him down. At the same time it felt as though a hand had pressed itself over his mouth and pinched his nose, so that the best he could do was struggle and go, 'Oof!' Then his finger was dragged out of his left ear and the whispering voice hissed, more urgently than before, 'Nicky, I need your help. Honest. Please! Listen . . . I'm stuck!'

Grover, seated in the desk directly in front of Nicky, swung round in his chair. He saw the Willybeast, saw Nicholas Chew thrashing about, and gave him a look meaning, 'God, Chew, you're asking for it, aren't you, drawing that?'

As if this were not bad enough, Grover suddenly shot to his feet and gave a howl of pain, grasping his backside and jumping up and down in the aisle.

'Christopher!' cried Mr Purvis. 'What on earth . . . ?'

'Chew kicked me, sir! Really hard, right up the backside!'

Nicky was horrified. 'I didn't, sir. How could I? I'm miles away from him, sir. Ask Aziz.' But his words were drowned in the general uproar.

'Freeze!' yelled Mr Purvis. He sat at the teacher's desk, his fingers poised on its surface as if he were about to play the organ. 'I will not have this nonsense!' he cried. 'I have never—'

The class never found out what Mr Purvis had never— instead, his head threw itself back, but not in one of his normal theatrical gestures. No, this was something quite new. It was just as if somebody had grasped hold of the few long hairs that still sprouted from the back of his head and given them a powerful yank. A second later, Mr Purvis *whacked* his forehead on the desk, and as he pushed himself up with his hands, the class saw that somehow he had managed to push two marker pens, one green and the other red, right up his nostrils.

The bell went loudly, triggering spontaneous and generous applause from the majority of the class before they piled out for their lunch. Oh, he was a laugh, that Mr Purvis! Carter stayed behind, as usual, and volunteered to collect the papers. He was surprised that Nicholas Chew refused to hand his in and more surprised to see him screw it up and put it into his pocket. This Carter reported to the still-seated Mr Purvis, to whom Grover was complaining bitterly about being attacked from the rear. Finally it dawned on him that his idol was still looking a bit groggy, even though he had pulled the pens from his nose. 'Are you feeling all right, sir?' he enquired.

'A little faint, actually, Chris. I wonder if you could just see me down to the staffroom. I could do with a glass of water.'

'Right you are, sir,' said Grover, bending to help Mr Purvis to his feet. There was a thud as their heads clashed together, for all the world as if somebody had got hold of them and slammed them together like a pair of cymbals. Nicholas watched open mouthed as the pair of them staggered to their feet, holding their battered skulls.

'Ouch! Sorry, sir! What happened? You OK? We must have slipped.'

On the whiteboard behind the pair, words began to form in red board marker.

Feed the fish . . . JBL

JBL? Was that somebody's initials or the Junior Biology Lab? There was a fish tank in the Junior Lab, certainly, and as an official Lab Monitor, Nicky did sometimes feed them.

The words shone for a second until Mr Purvis's handkerchief rose of it own accord and wiped them away. The classroom door opened and closed itself.

'Don't think you're getting away with this, Chew,' hissed Grover, leading away the staggering Mr Purvis, as if from a battle zone. 'You wait, I'll have you later!'

11. Big Hugs

Mr Purvis wasn't quite his cocky old self as he tucked into steak and chips with gravy in the haven of the Staff Dining Room. Still, by the time he got into his banana and custard, he was blahing away and interrupting all the other teachers' conversations with annoying puns and old jokes, as usual. 'Banged me poor old coconut while giving my all to 7R3,' he said loudly, rubbing his forehead. 'But at least I didn't have to put up with that nitwit Gasper! He did a bunk today, trying to dodge my test, you see, the poor deluded little fool! He's so stupid he thinks he can pull a fast one on me – but he's going to find out the hard way that Gasper the Exasperator has had his last gasp!'

The head and shoulders of his neighbour at the table, Mr McBrien, assistant French teacher, were vibrating like a tumble-dryer. He had heard the Exasperator joke a dozen times before, but he was anxious to show that he was 'exactly on the same wave length, humour-wise' (his expression) as his Head of Department, Mr Purvis. He chuckled away merrily until his own bananas and custard suddenly went mad and flipped themselves over him, sliding down his cardigan before gathering into a warm yellow pool in his lap. 'My goodness, Ronnie,' he said, trying to keep smiling while he scooped banana and custard off his crotch with his spoon, 'these bananas seem to have a life of their own.'

'Well something seemed to *put the skids* under them, eh, Patrick?' quipped Mr Purvis, pleased with his terrible pun.

A fork removed itself from the table and hovered behind Mr Purvis's seat. Its sharp little prongs quivered in anticipation. They were poised to *put the skids* under Mr Purvis. But the fork was distracted from its puncturing purpose by the sudden and flustered arrival of Mademoiselle Gasquet, the French *Assistante*, known to all the boys as Fifi. The fork replaced itself on the table. The high heels of Mlle Gasquet, a short and very attractive young woman, clacked menacingly towards the top table until she was standing roughly where the fork had hovered a moment before. She demanded to speak to Mr Purvis urgently. She looked agitated.

'Well, you know, I haven't quite finished my lunch, my dear,' he said importantly. 'Can't it wait?'

'Better not,' said Mlle Gasquet grimly. 'For your sake.' She spun round and clacked back towards the door.

Mr Purvis scowled a disapproving smile and whispered to the still-scooping Mr McBrien that the poor love didn't always get her English quite right and what could she be fussing about, *ooh la la*? Then he followed her out of the dining room and along the corridor. Past the library they rushed, click clack, into the staffroom, Mr Purvis humming loudly all the way to show how unconcerned he was, though in truth he was feeling curiously unsettled this morning. Stiffly, she led him to a gathering of armchairs apart from the others and motioned for him to sit. They were both far too preoccupied to notice the imprint of a third bottom forming itself in the cushion of the chair next to them.

''Ow dare you!' hissed Mlle Gasquet.

Mr Purvis made calming gestures. She was being a little too loud for comfort.

'What is it? What's upset you?'

'It is beastly! I make my way into ze toilet of the ladies. Zat is a private place! So 'ow dare you to come and make a tapping on ze door and say zose zings to me?'

'What things, Madeleine? I mean I would never . . .'

'You know very well what zings. You say you fancy me desperately. You say I am your Fifi! You say to meet me behind ze tennis court for snoggings!'

'Please, Madeleine, I beg you. Keep your voice down. *Me?* Tapping on a toilet door? This is nonsense! Who said those things to you?'

'I know zat voice! It belongs to you, a married man! And in a toilet, too! Zat is a disgrace! It is 'arassment!'

The silence elsewhere in the room was so intense that it was obvious to Mr Purvis that every other member of staff was straining to listen. But even the most acute of ears missed the sound of writing and suppressed giggles coming from a table close by.

On the table under the window next to the door, a pile of marking awaited Mlle Gasquet. On the top of the pile was Mlle Gasquet's mark book. The front cover of this mark book was quite plain – at least it had been until this moment when words began to write themselves in red biro and in large capital letters. The unseen hand finished with three extra-large kisses:

FIFI DARLING, I BURN FOR YOU.
HUGS, MY LOVE.
RONNIE P. XXX
(PS. TAP TAP!)

Then the staffroom door seemed to blow open and foot-steps were heard, heading in the direction of the Junior Biology Lab.

12. A Pact

It would be wrong to describe Nicky's state as he fed the tropical fish in the Junior Biology Lab with desiccated daphnia as nervous. Even an angelfish or a guppy or a neon could tell by the over-generous helpings of dried insects scattered upon the surface of their weedy, bubbling world, that the hand that fed them was shaking like a leaf.

Nicky had never really felt comfortable being alone with so many jars of pickled rat, so many coiling organs trapped in plastic moulds, so many creatures writhing in tanks; even though he was an official lab monitor, licensed to hang about here when others had to brave the perils of the cold and screaming playground. Imagine how he felt, then, waiting for that disembodied voice to pour itself into his ear again. Three times he told himself he was OK, he wasn't going to die.

Something caught his eye on the far side of the lab. The skeleton in the corner, hanging from its hook, lifted its arm and waved. He froze. Down went the skeleton's arm and up went the legs. '*Daahh da-da diddle da-da diddle diddle . . .*' It was singing the cancan!

Nicky didn't scream. Maybe it was because the crazy skeleton business was somehow less terrifying than the threat of more close-up whispering. He crossed and uncrossed the fingers of both hands. One, two, three.

Then he spoke as levelly as he could. 'Wh . . . who are you and what do you want?'

'Silence in court!' said the skeleton in the voice of Mr Maggs, his Biology teacher. Its jaws were going now, and it came out with another of Mr Maggs's famous sayings. 'Window open, can't stand the smell!' Then it added in a different voice, a boy's voice, one that Nicky thought he recognized, 'Let me hear you say that.'

'Window open, can't stand the smell,' repeated Nicky, his heart racing.

There followed a series of shrieking sounds, as if someone in trainers were rushing towards him over the polished floor. The air stirred in front of him for a second. Immediately after that, the window to his left unlatched and flung itself wide open, and the last bit of spit in Nicky's mouth dried up.

'Now say, "Lights on".'

Again, Nicky obeyed. The lights flicked on by themselves. Then off. The voice was horribly close now.

'Clever boy. You have extrasensory powers. Now hold out your right hand.'

Nicky put out his hand as a person who is nervous of dogs puts out his hand to a Rottweiler. He felt it grasped by warm, firm fingers.

'Sorry about that. Couldn't resist it. Hello, Nicky, it's me, Oliver. What did you think of my Maggsie impression? Good, eh?'

Nicky tried but couldn't speak.

'Don't be scared, I'm not dead or anything. Just . . . in another state of being, sort of.'

Nicky nodded. It seemed to be the thing to do.

'I need you to help me. I can't get back,' said the voice, and another hand gripped Nicky's outstretched hand. 'I'm not kidding now. Can you help me, please? I'm Oliver.'

'Oliver?' echoed Nicky. 'Oliver Gasper? What are you . . . what's happened to you?'

Oliver told him the story. He felt pressed by the fact that Mr Maggs might come in at any second, but he gave a pretty clear account of the article he'd read on the way to Reginald Pugh's; he told about Reggie ripping his dad off, and how he was so desperate to miss school, he'd managed, after loads and loads of false starts and failures, to focus his mind and recite the 'auspicious' words thirty-three times plus three plus three. Naturally, that last bit with all the threes in it struck a chord with Nicky. Oliver's most urgent point was that he needed somebody (a) to help him get his dad's property back because every penny counted at the moment and (b) to help him get back to normal. And he thought Nicky was the best person to do that.

'I think I get what you're saying,' said Nicky, looking at him – well, looking in the direction he thought he might be in – with what Oliver discovered were indeed wide blue eyes. 'But what I don't get is why you don't just go back to Stourley and take whatever you like from that antiques chap yourself. How could he stop you? And then you can make yourself visible again by reversing those words you had to say. You've just told me that's what the professor said the holy men did in India.'

'You don't get it, do you? I copied those words onto

the back of me hand, remember? Now I'm invisible, I can't see them, can I? I can't even remember what they were the right way round, let alone backwards. Except for *juldi*, I think it was.'

'Oh.'

'And how'm I going to travel thirty-plus kilometres each way, find the magazine with the words in it, plus drag two boxes of stuff out of the shop without a bit of help, eh? Look, for a start you've got no idea what it's like being invisible. People think you can just do anything you like – but you want to try getting on a bus when nobody can see you, like I did this morning. Feel that!'

Nicky felt his hand being pulled upwards, to where Oliver's head must be when he was standing. He lifted the other hand and began to feel the outline of the face. When he felt cheekbones under his thumbs, he could feel Oliver pulling back.

'Careful! The woman on the seat next to me gave me a right hammering with her elbow. I bet I've got a black eye. Plus I got smacked by a folded pushchair. Here, just here – feel this lump.' Nicky ran his palm over the invisible hair, found the (sticky-out) ear, the roundness of the skull – and then a lump like the proverbial egg.

Oliver told him how he nearly got killed at a crossing, even when the lights were against the traffic, because a van driver thought there was no one around. 'So I need a minder,' he explained earnestly. 'I know I've been mucking about, but I'm really scared, I don't mind telling you. It was 'orrible getting here and I don't fancy travelling back on my own. Everything's so weird – like, you can't even *find* anything. I mean, everything I had on me when I made myself invisible – that's invisible now too. Wait, hold your hand out and I'll show you.'

Nicky could hear Oliver rustling in his pockets.

'That's me bus pass, right?'

Something flat, oblong and sharp at the corners was placed in his palm. 'Could be,' said Nicky.

'This is me chewing gum, yeah?'

'Yes. I can smell it.'

'Pen, tissue . . .'

'Yuk!' said Nicky.

'And me mobile. That's the lot.'

'Let me see it – feel it, I mean,' said Nicky. His fingers closed round the invisible phone. He ran his finger and thumb over its tapered edges, felt the smooth surface of the screen and, lower down, the raised buttons of the keypad. The little machine was still warm from Oliver's invisible pocket. He handed it back. Then he thought for a minute before he said, 'This is weird. Things you touch now, they don't disappear, do they?'

'Only stuff I eat and drink,' said Oliver. 'But when I had a pee, I couldn't see that. Please. You gotta help me.'

'OK but why me?' said Nicky. 'It's not as if I'm your friend or anything.'

'Well, who else am I gonna ask, eh?' said Oliver. 'I haven't got any friends either. Sorry, I don't mean to say *you* haven't got any . . . Well you haven't, have you . . . ? Anyway, what I'm saying is, everybody in school thinks I'm an idiot, right?'

'Well, you do tend to muck about all the time . . .'

'Yeah, and everybody takes the mick all the time – but not you. And besides . . .' Nicky felt his sleeve being tugged. 'Look, don't take this as an insult or anything, cos you're brainy and everything, but nobody ever notices you, do they? You know how to keep your head down. You've got what they call a low profile, haven't you? So you could get away with covering for me.'

'So what you're saying is,' whispered Nicky, lowering his eyes, 'I could be useful to you because I'm invisible, too. That's it, isn't it?'

He got a gentle punch in the arm by way of a reply, and then Oliver said, 'I never thought of that. But hey, that's good, that is. Gasper and Chew, the Invisible Two. Sounds well smart, doesn't it? Goes together lovely! And I'll tell you what. When we find that magazine, you can have a go at the real thing, eh? I'm talking about disappearing, yeah? Only if you want to, though. But listen! It's brilliant in some ways – getting away with things – like giving Grover a good kick up the bum. And I mean, how else could I have dropped old Purvis in it with Fifi? Oh, you don't know about that, do you? I'll tell you about that later. But hey, what about the way I got my own back on him in class, eh? You saw that, didn't you? Talk about a laugh!'

Nicky pulled the screwed-up test paper out of his pocket and unfolded it until the Willybeast appeared. 'And this was your idea of a good laugh, too, then?' he said.

'Cool!' said Oliver. You could practically hear him grinning.

'Thanks a lot,' said Nicky. 'Before you decided to be my friend, I was on perfectly good terms with Mr Purvis and Chris Grover. Now they're both going to kill me.'

'Not if you do what you normally do and keep your head down!' said Oliver. 'You just go along to your lessons like a good little Nicky and everything will be cool. Then later on, we'll go round your house and do a bit of planning, eh? Can we? Go on, please. Because if you won't help me – that's it – I could be stuck like this forever.'

'OK, I'll help you,' said Nicky, hearing a note of real desperation in Oliver's voice. 'But don't come embarrassing me again in lessons, OK?'

'All right, all right! I won't, I promise. I've got plenty of other things I can do, you know.' Nicky heard him moving along the lab and the squeal of a stool that he nudged on his way past. Then the trainer squeaks stopped and there was a snort of laughter. 'Here, I've just thought. We better not call ourselves The Invisible Two. T-I-T, get it? So how about The *Unvisible* Two – THE TUTS? Yeah? Or maybe The Unvisibles? That's it, that's the one! We'll be "The Unvisibles"! See yuh!'

'See you,' said Nicky automatically.

'Oh no you won't, mate,' chuckled an echoing voice. Oliver must have nipped out into the corridor. 'Not unless you help me get back!'

13. Revenge is Sweet

It was a huge relief for Oliver to have a minder. The panic he'd felt in the shed when he realized he couldn't assemble the right words to get him back to normal had been the worst feeling in his life. That was closely followed by the near-miss with the van and the accidental battering he'd got from the other passengers on the bus. That had scared him badly, making him realize how dangerous the outside world could be when nobody can see you. But now he was in school and had Nicky's word that he'd help, he felt a bit safer, a bit more in control.

He decided, when he left Nicky in the lab, that the most important thing for him to do was to get hold of 7R3's register and mark himself in as present for the day. He reckoned that once he'd done this, with a bit of luck, Mr Stevens his form teacher wouldn't remember in a couple of weeks when he'd been 'missing', so there wouldn't be any awkward questions to answer at school or at home. However, as he stepped out into the corridor, the bell went for afternoon registration, so he was forced to take refuge in the dining hall to avoid colliding with a hundred hurrying bodies.

A couple of ladies were clearing up after dinner, clattering plates and cutlery on to a trolley. Oliver moved past, tapping one on the shoulder and grinning to himself as she swivelled round to see what her friend wanted, only to discover that her friend was up at the other end of the table. He tiptoed to the serving counter where the manageress, Mrs Stickley, was checking the takings in the till. Standing only a few metres from her, Oliver helped himself to a bag of Maltesers, silently ripping off the corner and tumbling them into his mouth. She was too engrossed to notice the round, chocolate balls floating for a second in space before they vanished, or the self-crumpling wrapper that tossed itself into the bin. Oliver ran his thumbnail between the ribs of a bar of KitKat with an expert slicing movement and popped chocolate chunks into his cheek. He timed the ripping of a Lion Bar packet so that it was drowned by the crash of cutlery into a sink in the kitchen behind him. He moved behind the counter and washed the stickiness down with a stream of Irn-Bru that he sucked straight from the tap of the cooling machine. He felt weird about all this – knowing it was wrong – but at the same time it was thrilling to have the power to take what he wanted from under the nose of the woman who had sent him to the back of the queue the day before for trying to shove in. It gave him an appetite to see what else he could get away with. It also made him start thinking who else he could get his own back on.

Five minutes later, the bell went for the first lesson of the afternoon, and while Nicky was back in class, finding out for the first time in his life what it was like not to be able to concentrate on what he was supposed to be doing (which was Geography with Mr Tranter), Oliver was hanging about outside the secretary's office. A senior boy called Watson came hurrying along the corridor with an armful of sixth-form registers. He was Vice Captain of Oliver's House and had made Oliver turn up for cross-country practice even when it was pouring with rain. Out went Oliver's foot just as Watson stepped through the office door. 'What the . . . Sorry, Mrs Higgins. The carpet must have got rucked up,' he stammered, picking himself up off the floor by her feet.

Oliver was just about to trip him up again on the way out when he thought he might try something else instead – so, as Watson went past, he flicked his ear. 'Ow!' Watson spun round, glaring.

'Damn and blast it to hell!' blurted Oliver in a voice very much like Watson's that echoed down the corridor.

'What on earth has got into you, Nigel?' hissed Mrs Higgins, dashing out to confront him. 'Swearing like that! Sixth formers are supposed to set an example to the rest of the school!'

She ignored Watson's protest of innocence and followed him out into the corridor. She had a real go at him before sending him off with a different sort of flea in his ear. Oliver popped into her office feeling very satisfied with himself. Mrs Higgins followed a moment later, muttering to herself about kids today; she started flipping the sixth-form registers into their slots in the top drawer of one of the filing cabinets. When she'd done that, she began to check that all the registers had been returned. When she got to Year 7, she worked her way through. 7R1, 7R2 . . . '7R3? Missing! I might have guessed . . .' she said aloud. Hurrying footsteps along the corridor announced the late arrival of Warburg.

'Mr Tranter's apologies, Mrs Higgins,' squeaked

Warburg, blinking up at her. 'He asked me to say, and I quote, "Enthusiasm for matters geographical temporarily distracted him from his other duties". He hopes you will forgive him.'

'Blooming cheek!' laughed Mrs Higgins and patted Warburg's brainy head. Oliver was disgusted to see that she thought he was sweet. 'Anyone absent?' she asked affectionately.

'Gasper, Miss.'

'That dreadful ginger-haired boy? The noisy one who's always in trouble?'

'That's the one, Miss. The one with the ears. He's always skiving off. He's just trying to get out of a French test this time.'

Oliver wet his lips, put out his invisible tongue and released a long, low farting sound. Mrs Higgins and Warburg froze, each eyeing the other with total disbelief.

'I *beg* your pardon?' said Mrs Higgins after a moment of silence.

'Oh, that's all right,' murmured Warburg, holding up his hand to show that he understood, really he did.

'No it is *not* all right,' said Mrs Higgins firmly. 'Manners!'

'Never mind,' whispered Warburg, a bit awkward but trying to be helpful. 'It's quite a natural response of the digestive system. Did you happen to have any sort of cabbage or beans for lunch? My mother suffers dreadfully with wind after anything like that.'

'What are you talking about? Are you suggesting that I made that frightful . . . I mean . . .'

Warburg stood frozen to the spot with embarrassment

for a second. 'Must rush,' he said hastily. 'See you tomorrow, Mrs Higgins.' As he retreated, Oliver let rip with another reverberating raspberry. This was too much for Warburg; he totally lost his cool and suddenly shot off down the corridor like a human cannonball.

Mrs Higgins, red as a beetroot, opened her mouth to call after him but thought better of it when she noticed that a light was flashing on her telephone. The Head wanted her. She snatched up a notepad and swept through the door into his office, full of righteous indignation.

Oliver flipped open 7R3's register and found the most recent entries against his name: *a* for absent, morning and afternoon. He reached for Mrs Higgins's Tippex, deciding to do something about it. The stuff was runnier than he anticipated and spread over some of the grid lines. He groaned quietly, knowing that he'd almost certainly made things worse. It was only a matter of time before Mr Stevens would notice the mess, and he would be bound to suspect Oliver of forgery. He consoled himself with the thought that he might never be seen again, in which case, what did anything matter?

After that, he decided to kill time by having a good nose about. As Mrs Higgins bustled out of the Head's room, he popped in through the open door. Remembering his last end of term report with the stern warnings that the Head had added, Oliver amused himself by leaning across his desk until he was practically nose to nose with him. While the Head checked through a letter on his desk and prepared to sign it, Oliver ran through his repertoire of rude and insulting faces and gestures.

Mr Dollis, blissfully unaware of this, leaned back and picked his nose, examining the result and rolling it thoughtfully between finger and thumb.

'Urgh,' said Oliver. He was a great nose-picker himself but he was genuinely shocked to see what the Head got up to in private. His outburst shook Mr Dollis into a startled cry of, 'Ahh!' and made him twitch like mad. When he was calmer, having gazed all about to make sure that he had only *imagined* hearing somebody say 'Urgh!', he pulled open a drawer and took comfort in a Twix. He bit into one of the bars, licked his lips, looked at his watch, stretched and then went off to answer a call of nature. Oliver scoffed the rest of the biscuits while he was gone and relished the puzzled, frustrated look on the Head's face when he came back in again and sat down. Mr Dollis scratched his head, then he started searching rapidly through all the drawers, opening and slamming them shut one after the other. 'Margery . . . ?' he called, exasperated.

'Yes?' called Mrs Higgins.

'What happened to my . . . ? Did you just . . . ?'

'I beg your pardon, Mr Dollis?'

'Never mind.' The Head dropped to his knees and peered under his desk. As he did so, Oliver slid out the plastic drawer from under the top of the desk.

BLAM! Mr Dollis's skull hit the underside of the drawer with a crack that scattered pens and pencils, paper clips and staples over a wide area. After that, Oliver had the pleasure of watching him, and then Mrs Higgins, crawling over the carpet, searching for all the bits and pieces like a couple of grazing sheep. The temptation presented by two such targets to an invisible boy with several grudges was too strong to resist. The side-footer that he applied to the Head's rear end was quite a gentle one under the circumstances, but it left him gaping like a goldfish at Mrs Higgins. Then, before he could accuse her of foul play, she suddenly clutched her behind, leaped to her feet shouting, 'Mister Dollis!' and dashed back to her office.

Unfortunately for Oliver, Mrs Higgins's way of dealing with this shocking business was to throw herself into her work, so his delight was quickly cut short a few minutes later, when he heard her leaving a message on his parents' answerphone. 'Message for Mr and Mrs Gasper,' she said. 'Mrs Higgins speaking, school secretary, Honnington House. Just a reminder that it's school policy to alert parents when boys are absent without prior notice and when there are grounds for concern. So we'd be very grateful if you'd call us, just to confirm that everything is in order. Thank you. Goodbye.'

Oliver had to think fast. Mum and Dad were away, but what about Carrie? She might wander in from the shop and listen to the messages. Probably not, though, at least not before Oliver was home from school. Automatically he raised his hand to look at his watch and saw . . . nothing . . . but the clock on the wall told him that there was quite a while to go before the end of school.

The key to the house was kept in the shop behind the counter, right under Carrie's nose. Chances were that, if the shop was empty, she'd notice a key suddenly flying off by itself as he tried to smuggle it out. Besides, he couldn't just phone up and tell her he was staying out all night. She wouldn't have that – and she'd probably tell Mum and Dad he was mucking her about! No, he'd have to get Nicky to come along in person and charm her into thinking it was all *his* idea to invite Oliver to stay over at his house.

If only he could go and explain to Nicky right now – but Nicky had warned him to leave him alone in lessons.

He wandered along the empty corridors, wishing he could hurry school along. Deciding that he couldn't, he did what he usually did when faced with a problem: tried to forget it by mucking about. He looked in on Mrs Higgins's bog to see if there was anything more exciting about it than the Staff Ladies' bog. There wasn't. Still, he put the seat up so that she would wonder if the Head had popped in for a quick tinkle and set off in search of other places where he wasn't normally allowed to go.

The Sixth Form Common Room was a disappointment, with only a few tame pin-ups on the lockers. There were a couple of sixth formers in there, on a free period. 'Lucky dogs!' thought Oliver. One was yawning his head off as he leafed idly through a magazine. The other was tapping a ping-pong ball off a table and against the wall. Oliver didn't know either of them. Still, as far as he was concerned, sixth formers generally gave kids his age a hard time, so he caught the ping-pong ball on the rebound, popped it into the yawner's wide-open mouth and shouted, 'What a shot!' He didn't bother to stay for the argument.

Pushing open classroom doors and nosing about in the private offices of various heads of department wasn't terribly exciting after a while, so he made his way to the sports hall to see if there was anything more interesting going on there. A noisy, blundering game of basketball was in session between two Year 9 teams. A weedy looking boy was jumping up and down in an unmarked position within shooting range of the basket when Oliver launched himself into the game. 'Pass! Pass, Robbo! Oh come on! Why don't you ever pass to me?' he whined.

'Because you're useless!' panted Robbo, a thick-set, tall kid with a number three crop who had always run rings round Oliver on the basketball court. There was no doubt that he had a talent for the game. He skipped past three defenders, turning and shielding the bouncing ball, looking for another teammate to pass to. Seeing nobody else in front, apart from the weedy boy, he flipped the ball stylishly back over his shoulder, intending it for another attacking player he knew to be just behind him. Oliver moved in silently, leaped and intercepted the pass. He ran the other way with the ball, bounced it off the head of the attacker Robbo meant to pass to, caught it again and carried it back to Robbo's team's basket where he flipped it neatly through the hoop.

It was hard to tell which was louder, the mocking hoots of laughter from the opposition or the howls of rage from Robbo's teammates. 'Who's useless now?' yelled Oliver, adding his own voice to the barrage of insults.

Next stop, the swimming pool. Oliver was just about

to take the usual route, via the boys' changing rooms, when he realized that there was nothing to stop an invisible person entering by the door marked STAFF ONLY that led directly to the poolside at the shallow end. The noise in the steamy cavern of a place was deafening, what with the thunderous crash of the swimmers' arms and legs in the water and the reverberating yells of the rest of the class who lined up along the side to his right, jeering, shivering and jumping up and down, waiting for their turn. Mr 'Crusher' Thomas, Head of Sports Ed., was parading along the opposite side in his college tracksuit, stepping back every now and then to avoid even the slightest splashes. He liked to keep his kit looking smart, and he was proud of having a nickname that made him sound hard. The racers thrashed their way to the far end and the leaner, fitter ones began to heave themselves out of the water. Mr Thomas's whistle shrilled again.

'Back you go! One more length! Backstroke this time!' he yelled.

'Not fair, sir! No way, sir! You cannot be serious, sir!' gasped the ones in the water.

'What about us, sir? It's our go, sir! We're freezing!' (This from the boys turning blue on the side facing him.)

'Wait, you lot!' he shouted, enjoying their misery. He blew the whistle to stir the boys in the water into action again. As they began their slow, churning progress, he made a pushing gesture at the standing boys, indicating that they must keep well away from the side of the pool. 'You're not cold!' he jeered. 'Stop acting like a load of babies!'

'Here we go,' said Oliver to himself and he worked

his way down the line until, one after the other, he had shoved all the standing boys into the water. Normally Mr Thomas moved slowly with what he considered to be a panther-like coolness, but on this occasion, he was round the other side of the pool in a flash, purple in the face and blowing his whistle fit to bust.

'What the hell do you think you're doing?' he screamed at the seething mass of kids who were coughing and barking and blaming one another in the water. 'Get out! Get out now, all of you! Don't you realize how *dangerous* that sort of behaviour is?'

The pool was cleared in record time. Nobody messed with Mr Thomas. He herded them against the wall while he stood with his back to the pool, and started his lecture. 'Right, you clowns,' he said. 'It's pretty obvious to me that not one of you knows anything about basic safety procedures. Now whose bright idea was it for everybody to jump in? Come on, come on, own up!' Out came his trusty ref's notebook and pen. 'Nobody's going anywhere until I get a name. Do I make myself clea . . . AGHHH!'

Oliver only had to give him a bit of a shove in the chest and Crusher staggered backwards, his arms revolving like the sails of a windmill. His pen and notebook shot out of his grasp and away he went. He was only half aware of the marvellous *ker-sploonch* he made, but when he surfaced, he was greeted by two loud noises. One was a spontaneous burst of applause and the other was the ear-splitting, high-pitched pulse of the fire alarm.

14. Punch Up

Oliver had often wondered what it would feel like to lift the little steel hammer off its hooks below the fire-alarm box, smash the glass cover and press the red button. Now he knew: it felt great, especially when there was no way he could get caught. And there were a couple of bonuses.

(1) It could mean an early end to the school day.

(2) He guessed correctly that a stickler for the rules like Crusher Thomas would consider it his duty to '*move swiftly to the designated assembly point*' without pausing to change his dripping gear. And sure enough, there he was in a flash, in his soaking tracksuit, leading two lines of boys, wearing only their swimming trunks, *swiftly* into the main playground.

The plan backfired, however, because it took a good twenty-four minutes to do all the checks before anyone was allowed home – which turned out to be just about normal going-home time. So Oliver had to hang about too, worrying about how to deal with the answerphone message, while his class, as disappointed as he was not to be released before four o'clock, lined up grumpily alongside the rest of the classes assembled in the playground.

It crossed Nicky's mind, especially when he saw the state of Crusher Thomas and his swimming class, that

Oliver just might be behind this stunt, especially since it was timed so badly. Still, it also raised a faint hope that he might be able to slip quietly away without Chris Grover noticing. He'd brought his bag with him to the playground, assuming like most people that it was only a false alarm. And when at last the class, like a pack of unruly dogs, was let off the leash, he tried to blend with the crowd heading for the school gate. The normal Friday feeling in the air was tinged with niggle and frustration.

'Don't think you're getting out of it, Chew,' came Grover's commanding voice. 'Nobody boots my backside and gets away with it!' The boys surrounding Nicky made a channel for Grover to get through. 'I'll see you down the field. You'd better be there, that's all.' He swept off to collect his bag, followed by a chattering band of admirers who peeled themselves from the ranks of the homeward bound to join in the fun.

Immediately, Nicky was getting some very unwelcome attention. 'You've had it, Chewsy,' Jamie Robins told him, as if he didn't know.

'You want to just bring your elbows up like this,' said Ahluwalia, not unkindly. 'Then he can't smash you in the face.'

'Yeah, but what if Chris fights dirty?' said Bellamy. 'You'll probably get a knee in the wotsits. Aghhh!' He mimed what could happen and got a big laugh.

'Chris? He's not like that; he's a sportsman,' said Ahluwalia. 'Nah, he'll just smack you up a bit, show you he's the top man, like.'

Nicky drew very little comfort from this but he couldn't see how he could get out of being beaten to a pulp and still be able to hold his head up. The annoying thing was that this was Gasper's fight, not his – and where was he? Mucking about as usual, probably. Spying on people, probably; maybe he was emptying the school safe. Ridiculous. The whole thing was ridiculous . . . People just didn't become invisible. The writing on the whiteboard, the meeting in the lab – it all seemed so unlikely now and so long ago. He felt that there must be a rational explanation for it, hallucinations, perhaps, or maybe he was sickening for something, like when he had the fever with the flu that time.

Think, think, think. He made sure nobody was watching and turned round three times. They'd been doing Mahatma Gandhi, one of India's greatest political heroes, in PSRE. He had a very effective way of dealing with violence; what was it called? Passive resistance. You don't fight, you just stand still or lie down on the ground and let your enemies make all the moves. OK, he'd try that.

Robins, Bellamy and Ahluwalia sort of hung around him like prison warders and went with him down the south steps, the smokers' route at breaktimes. They cut past the tennis courts where Mehta and Babber were keeping a lookout for Nicky and dashed off, shouting when they saw him. Obviously they were going to warm up the crowd down between the back of the science block and the cricket nets. Nicky glanced at the empty nets and thought of the various squads who trained there, sometimes pitting themselves against the fearsome arm of Crusher Thomas and the cunning donkey drops of Mr Purvis. Nicky played for the Colts, just far enough down the batting order not to be expected to do anything spectacular. He thought of the way Chris Grover, his captain, stood unflinching against the worst that any bowler could heave at him, blocking and steering each ball with his steely wrists. So what chance had he got, even to land a blow on him?

Of the twenty or so blokes who had stayed to watch the fight, there wasn't one who doubted the outcome. They lined up along the wall to watch Chew get hammered, hoping it wouldn't take too long in case there was anything worth watching on telly. Mehta was holding Chris Grover's uniform jacket and was accepting his tie when Nicky appeared.

'Ah! You've turned up, then?' Grover said, sarcastically. 'Thought you might try to chicken out of it.' The heavy traffic on the road beyond the bushes meant he had to shout.

'I wish I knew what this was all about,' said Nicky, as calmly as he could, though his face was twitching.

'I don't like getting kicked, that's what it's all about. And don't try to deny you kicked me,' said Grover.

'I saw you jumping about, that's all,' said Nicky quietly. He tried to look calm by putting his hands behind his back, but his fingers seemed to have a will of their own; they crossed and uncrossed themselves, one-two-three, one-two-three.

'Can't hear you. Speak up,' said Grover, moving closer menacingly.

Nicky was still debating whether to say it again, when a voice, very much like his own and close behind him, called, 'Then you shouldn't go crawling to Mr Purvis and you shouldn't have such a fat arse!'

'Wha-a-at!' Furious, Grover charged at Nicky. He would have flattened him, coming at him as he did, like a train, but suddenly he measured his length on the grass, falling at Nicky's feet.

'Woah!' went the crowd. 'Steady, Chris!'

He was up quickly, but no sooner had he squared up to Nicky again, than he let out a shriek and spun round, his fists flying. 'Who did that? What coward did that?'

The crowd had gathered in a sort of horseshoe away from the wall of the bowling shed, but nobody was within a metre of either of the fighters. 'Wotcha talkin' about? Nobody touched you! Get on with it! Sort him out, Chris!' urged the crowd.

'Somebody kicked my bum!' roared Grover.

'So you keep saying,' said Nicky. It really was him speaking this time, not Oliver. He was surprised to hear some of the crowd laugh approvingly at this.

'That's it! You stand up to him, Nicky!' Could that be Robins taking his side?

Grover wasn't having any of this, and he caught Nicky completely off guard, rushing at him and knocking him down. In an instant, he had got him in a tight neck lock and was rolling over and over with him. Never having been in this situation before, all Nicky could do was try to tear Grover's arms away from his windpipe in order to get some air. But suddenly, Grover was staggering backwards on to his knees, yelling 'Leggo my hair! Fight fair!'

'I haven't touched your hair,' returned Nicky,

straightening himself up and brushing grass off his blazer three times. He took it off and held it out. Ahluwalia and Bellamy tussled for the right to hold it.

He abandoned passive resistance and ran at Grover, who put up his elbow and caught Nicky a glancing blow on the nose. It brought tears to Nicky's eyes, hurting enough to make him throw caution to the wind and start throwing his arms about like somebody who's just disturbed a wasps' nest. Grover seemed to expect this and jumped sideways but, as he did so, he felt the back of his knees come into contact with something solid. Later, when he had time to reflect, he would remember that it felt like an upholstered stool or maybe a big dog. Anyway, over he went, thumping his head on the ground. Before he could fend him off, Nicky was on his chest, pinning his arms down. And then, for some reason, he found he couldn't breathe. How Chew managed it, he couldn't figure out, but somehow he got a clever grip on him that made him feel as though he was being smothered with an enormous cushion. He would never know what had actually happened – that Oliver had sat on his head. Next thing he knew, there was Chew, standing with his back to him, punching the air to the crowd, which was screaming, 'Nick-ee! Nick-ee!'

Christopher Grover saw one last chance to regain a bit of lost dignity. He jumped up and took a leap at Chew, meaning to get him round the neck and drag him back to earth. Chew ducked at the last moment and then, as he made contact with Chew's shoulders, something seemed to lift Grover's legs and turn his body, so that he sailed over Chew's head and came down heavily on a pile of schoolbags that knocked the wind out of him as he landed. He hardly heard the countdown, but he was aware of twenty pairs of arms making the sign familiar to everyone who has ever watched wrestling on the TV – forearms crossed at chest level, followed by karate chops to both sides at once – meaning *You are well and truly OUT, man!*

Chris Grover was a good loser. He dragged himself to his feet and shook hands, congratulating Nicky on some ace moves. As for Nicky Chew, everybody said they never thought he had it in him. That was a fantastic throw, that last one. He heard Bellamy assuring Wells that he knew for certain that he had a black belt in karate but he wasn't the type to brag about it. He got his coat brushed for him, a tissue for his bloody nose, a helping hand with his rucksack, countless pats on the back and several offers to wait for him if he was catching the bus.

He thanked all his fans but no, he'd be all right, he had a couple of things to pick up from the Music School.

'Up the Unvisibles!' whisper-shouted the panting invisible comrade-in-arms who kept pace with Nicky as he pounded up the steps again. An unseen hand gave him a congratulatory pat on the back. 'Now let's get a shift on. We need to get to my place before Carrie picks up the answerphone messages – and you've got some fast talking to do.'

15. To Oliver's House

As a result of having run like mad to the request bus stop at Hatton Gardens, the Unvisibles managed to avoid travelling with the crowd from the fight, but they had, nonetheless, a far from peaceful journey on the 127 bus. A bunch of fourth formers wearing the uniform of St Benedict's High was already on board. Normally, Nicky would have blended into the background, perhaps reading his book or smiling politely as he ignored the suggestion that Honnington House was a rubbish school for losers.

By the time the bus had arrived at Royal Gardens, however, Nicky was beginning to feel the need for body armour rather than a background to blend into. Things were getting a bit lively in spite of the fact that Nicky had tried closing his eyes and blinking in threes. An enormous sports bag had mysteriously emptied itself on the head of the spottiest and loudest thug on the bus and, somehow, his spray can of 'Tough Guy Dry' deodorant went off by itself and deodorized the entire back row. Spotty Boy's mate received a swift backhander to the side of his head with an airborne badminton racquet. But things started getting really worrying for Nicky when a very large St Benedict's kid, evidently called Snag, started to come at him from the rear. Snag seemed bent on sorting Nicky out, even though he couldn't work out exactly how Nicky had carried out his bag-attack without making an obvious move from his seat halfway up the aisle.

Why Snag suddenly decided to throw himself across two lady passengers, nobody was able to say. It was unfortunate for him, since they had already made up their minds to make separate calls to St Benedict's head teacher complaining about rowdy behaviour on buses. Now the police seemed more appropriate and the bus driver started calling them on his radio.

So it was with some relief that Nicky reached his stop and was able to jump down the steps of the bus on to the relative calm of the pavement. Oliver was a little slow to get off but Nicky knew he wasn't far behind him; he heard him go 'Agh!' as he got clouted by the hissing automatic doors.

'Serves you right for provoking a riot,' said Nicky, guessing correctly that Oliver had been too busy looking behind him, enjoying the results of his mischief, to dodge the doors.

'Well, they asked for it,' said Oliver, still sounding cheerful as he came alongside. 'Now listen, mate. All you've got to do is tell Carrie I'm staying with you tonight and can she let you have my toothbrush and pyjamas – oh, and a coupla quid out the till? But you'll have to be dead smooth, like, cause she's got a bit of a temper on her.' He provided a brief and rather alarming description of his sister and of what she was like when roused.

'And what if she wants to know why you haven't come with me?' asked Nicky nervously.

'You tell her I'm still at school, in the middle of a game of football but I'll ring her later, yeah? But listen, the main thing is, you keep her talking in the shop while I nip in the house and delete the messages.'

'How're you going to get in?' said Nicky.

'She keeps the house key on a hook inside the shop, behind the counter. I'll lift it while you're distracting her.'

'Won't she get a bit suspicious, though? She's never even heard of me, has she?'

'I s'pose she might,' Oliver agreed, sounding worried. 'But you can think of something, can't you? Oh go on, please, otherwise I'm stuffed, aren't I?'

By now, they had come to the corner of Shelley Avenue. George Gasper and Son was only just across the road. Nicky could see Carrie through the glass of the shop door. She was sitting on the counter drinking a cup of tea and smoking a roll-up. She was dressed in a carefully slashed black vest, a teenie-weenie black skirt over fishnet stockings (one red, one lime green) and deadly square-toed boots. Her straight, coal-black hair had a purple streak and was close-shaven around the family ears; otherwise it just hung, some of it in her tea, some in her eyes. Around her neck she wore a spiky dog collar, and she was elaborately pierced in all kinds of places. When she saw him peering at her, she waved the drifting smoke aside like a curtain and stared angrily back.

'Good luck, mate!' said Oliver.

'Make sure you hurry up and get the key once we're inside,' said Nicky firmly out of the side of his mouth to Oliver. 'Then go and sort out the messages. I don't want you standing listening to me telling lies for you.' He twisted the handle three times, pushing the door open.

As soon as he entered the shop, Carrie's surly expression melted. 'Hello, darlin',' she said sweetly. 'Lookin' for anything in particular?' She gestured towards the racks of plates, coronation mugs and salt and pepper pots and jugs, the knick-knacks, the pine chairs and tables and chests and wardrobes, the photograph frames, the shooting sticks, the garden tools and bird tables and concrete cupids. 'Somebody's birthday, is it?'

'Hi, I'm Nicky Chew,' said Nicky, extending his hand as boldly as he could. 'From next door, actually. You're Carrie, aren't you?'

'Got it in one, sweetheart,' smiled Carrie, surprised to be offered his hand and looking at it fondly, as though it were something cute, like a nice little hamster, maybe.

'Oh, that's good,' said Nicky. 'Because I was wondering . . .'

'You *are* from next door, int ya! I thought I recognized you from somewhere! So how come we never see you hardly? Hey, and you go to Honnington House, don't you? D'you know my little toe-rag of a brother?' interrupted Carrie.

'Well, I . . .' Nicky was rather taken aback.

'Come to think of it, you're not his sort, are you? You've got some manners for a start. Nice way of speaking, too, and all smart in your uniform – apart from that bit of a grass stain on your knees. Oh, and you've hurt your nose! What did you do, fall over? Shame! Come to think of it, I'm not surprised you steer well clear of

Oliver. Cheeky little so-and-so, he is. Got about as much sense and manners as a . . .'

'. . . a Neanderthal?' suggested Nicky quickly.

'Exactly! Thank you, Nicky. Just the word I was lookin' for.'

'Well, yes, as a matter of fact, I do know him. We're . . . um . . . friends, actually.'

'Wow! How come he's never mentioned you, then?'

'Well, um . . .' Nicky was aware of a key dangling just a few centimetres away from Carrie's belt-buckle. It suddenly rose from its hook and floated in a series of loops across the room. He tried not to stare as it slipped out of the open door and disappeared round the corner. 'It's . . . we've only. It's . . . we've only got to know each other lately, you see,' he stammered. 'But we get on . . . you know . . . really well. And anyway, the reason I dropped by was to say, um, Oliver's staying over with us tonight.'

'What!' Sheer disbelief that her brother had a friend made her open her mouth, revealing the stud through her tongue.

'Well, that's to say, we were rather hoping it would be OK with you if he stopped over with me. We're . . . sort of um . . . partners, in a way. We're working on a Topic together. Er . . . for PSRE. It's on – Gandhi, as a matter of fact . . .' Nicky was running out of steam. *Tap, tap, tap* went his foot, three times.

'Wait a minute, woah! You want our Oliver to come over to your house and *study*? You want him to *do some work* on Gandhi? Flippin' heck! That's a bit of a turn-up!'

'Yes, well, it's true,' he said lamely. 'I've come to pick up his pyjamas and . . .'

Carrie was out of her chair and pressing her lip-rings to his cheeks. He half realized he was being kissed, though it felt a bit like getting tapped with a curtain rod. 'You little darlin'!' she squealed. 'You are *gorgeous*! Thank you so much! That means I don't have to babysit! Here . . .' She gestured to a door behind her. 'Go through there into the house. Use this . . .' Her hand moved towards the hook behind the counter. 'Hey! That's weird! What's happened to the house key?' Her face collapsed in on itself as she concentrated. 'Never mind, use this one.' She produced a large bunch of keys from her pocket, holding up the sharp end of a shiny, brass Yale one. 'Here. Open the front door with this, go through the living room, then up the stairs. You want the second door on the left, next to the bathroom. Got it? That's Oliver's bedroom. OK? Ignore the smell, the mess and the football posters. You can find his jimjams, can't you? They're in there somewhere. And the blue toothbrush is his one – hardly used, yeah? Catch you in a bit.'

Her mobile was in her hand and a number was pip-ping away, *pip-pip-pip-pip*, as she spoke. 'Charlie? That you, Charlie, my darlin'? Carrie here. Yes it is, stop muckin' about. Listen, you're never going to believe this. You know I said I couldn't go down the Arts Centre wiv yah? Yeah, stuck wiv my brother and that. Well, guess what! He's sleepin' over wiv his little friend! Handy or what? Yeah! So pick me up at eight and don't be late, right? What d'you mean, you left me a nice long sloppy message on the answerphone? What, on the house answerphone? Oh, you big old softy! Yeah. No,

I'll go and have a listen straight away. Big kiss, babe, see you tonight. Bye!'

Nicky was still in the enormous, cluttered living room and starting to feel very nervous when Carrie finished her call and came through from the shop. He could hear the tinny voice of a recorded message clearly now, coming through the open door of the kitchen beyond. It was obviously taking Oliver longer to delete the messages than he'd anticipated. If the message from Carrie's boyfriend went on and on, chances were that the message from Mrs Higgins about Oliver's absence was still on the tape!

Still purring with pleasure and poking him playfully with the aerial of her mobile, Carrie said, 'Are you lost?' Nicky was certainly lost for words because she went on, 'You're a bit of all right, you are. Pity you're not ten years older because you are a bit of a gorgeous little gent, yeah?' Wink, wink.

Suddenly she became aware of the sound from the kitchen and started heading in that direction.

'I, um, I like that little tattoo on your shoulder,' said Nicky loudly, desperate to stall her.

Carrie stopped. 'Do you, love? Which one? You mean the snake or the writing?'

'Both,' said Nicky. 'They're very, um, intricate, aren't they? Did they hurt, having them done?'

'*Intricate*, eh? Ooh, you haven't half got a lovely way with words! You want to watch yourself, you, or you're going to be a bit of a good influence on my 'orrible little brother! Now come on, you nip up and get his pyjamas and stuff. The room past the bathroom, remember. I just want to hear what message my Charlie's left for me.'

She was moving quickly now and she was just in time to hear Mrs Higgins's official school-secretary voice saying '. . . so we'd be very grateful if you'd call us, just to confirm that everything is in order. Thank you. Goodbye.' Then immediately afterwards the phone display said, 'Message deleted.'

Carrie looked rather taken aback that the message had chosen to delete itself, but luckily she still seemed to have Charlie on her mind. 'I'll give him "confirm everything is in order"!' she giggled. 'He's such a fool, that Charlie Spencer. I bet he got his mum to say that for him!' She pressed the messages button. Nothing. Her expression became thunderous. 'What the . . . ? What's happened here? Nothing's happenin'!'

'Um it's probably static,' Nicky improvised, his heart pounding. His hand went quickly three times across his hair, stroke, stroke, stroke. 'If there's a magnetic build-up in the stratosphere it can play havoc with satellite communications.'

'Blimey!' said Carrie, impressed. Then she said, 'Shame, though. I was looking forward to hearin' Charlie getting all romantic. Never mind. You wait here and I'll nip upstairs and get Oliver's stuff for you, I might as well. Play yourself something on the jukebox if you like. In there.'

As she started up the stairs, Nicky stepped back into the Gaspers' spacious living room to where Carrie had pointed him. He was struck by the wonderful, colourful clutter of the place that contrasted so much with the quieter, smaller-scale, neatly ordered sparseness of his own house. He rather liked the cosy, shocking wall paper, bright with roses the size of cabbages, the shining shelf-loads of Victorian jugs and vases, the huge squashy sofa and armchairs, the glowing tank full of tropical fish. A fat-faced cat lay dozing on a litter of newspapers, magazines and comics. The *Sun* and the *News of the World* collided with heaps of *Beano, Hello!, Soccer Weekly* and *OK!* magazines; there was *Country Life, Antiques and Paintings, Viz, The Face, Pro Wrestling* and *Woman's Realm*. Why didn't they have any of these at his house? he wondered. A huge widescreen DVD telly and video squatted in one corner. The facing wall was taken over by a dresser, crowded with plates and dishes, not all the same pattern, but all of them in fabulous bright colours. Next to the French windows on the other side towered a massive, neon-lit Wurlitzer jukebox.

The air moved close by. 'Blimey, that was a near thing!' Nicky heard Oliver whisper. 'I like the bit about static – that was quick! But what have you been sayin' to her, mate? Normally she's 'orrible! She must fancy you or somethin'! Wah-hey!' Before Nicky could protest, he felt himself gripped by his wrists and pulled over to the fabulous record-machine. His left forefinger pressed itself on letter A and his right one on the number 24. The great rolling caterpillar of vinyl records revolved, the chrome arm engaged, clicked, tugged down a disc, turned it through ninety degrees and laid it on the already spinning turntable.

There was a sudden shout, a blare of saxophones, a thrash guitar.

Nicky found himself spun round and round to the rockin' rhythms of 'You Ain't Nuthin But a Hound Dog!' He was shoved backwards and forwards, his right arm thrown over his head. 'Let go! Pack it in, Oliver!' he panted. He did two wild jiving circuits of the room before he tripped over the rug and flew full length backwards on to the sofa, scattering mags and papers and sending the cat streaking for the kitchen cat flap. Carrie, who had just appeared with a Safeway bagful of her brother's overnight stuff wasn't quite quick enough to get out of the way. She got knocked sideways, skidded on the slippery cover of *Piercing News*, lost her balance and crashed on top of her visitor.

'I would never have taken you for an Elvis fan,' she chuckled, pushing herself off him and giving the squashed and mortified lad a heave-ho into the sitting position. 'You look more the Beethoven type.'

16. A Swing of the Starting Handle

'You are, aren't you – the Beethoven type?' Oliver asked as he and Nicky, the latter still sweaty with embarrassment, approached Nicky's front door a couple of minutes later. Nicky swung the plastic bag in what he hoped was the direction of Oliver's head, but he contacted nothing but empty air.

'Where are you?' he said.

'Right behind you, mate,' said Oliver, putting an invisible knee into the back of Nicky's thigh, though not hard enough to dead-leg him.

'Look,' said Nicky. 'If you want me to help you, you're going to have to stop mucking me about.'

'Did you ask her for some money?' interrupted Oliver. 'We're gonna need some for fares and food and that.'

'No,' said Nicky. 'How could I?'

'Never mind, I'll just have to nick some,' said Oliver, off-hand.

Nicky stopped dead so that Oliver walked into his back. 'If you do anything criminal, that's it, you're on your own.' Squeeze, squeeze, squeeze, went his fingers on the top of Oliver's arm to show he meant business.

'Well, who would know?'

'I would. And so would everybody else if they saw great wads of cash floating in the air . . .'

'Evening, Nicky? Talking to yourself?' The Unvisibles jumped. Over the fuchsia hedge that divided the drive of Number 30 from Nicky's front garden they saw a grinning Mr Dudzinski pop out from behind the raised engine cover of his sleek, dark blue 1929 Lancia Lambda. He was wearing enormous, oily rubber gloves.

'Oh, hello. Was I? Didn't realize,' said Nicky, feeling awkward.

'You OK? What happened to your nose? Did you fall over in the supermarket?' He nodded at the plastic bag in Nicky's hand.

'Ah,' said Nicky, as neutrally as he could.

Mr Dudzinski seemed happy with 'Ah' and moved on. 'You couldn't give us a hand with this, could you?' he said. 'I need to give this little tap half a turn. It's the petrol cut-off valve. If you don't close it when the car's standing on a slope, the petrol tends to leak out. I can manage a spanner all right, but this thing is killing my fingers.' He gave his wounded hands a waggle, then bent to point to the spot in the engine he was talking about.

Nicky and Oliver wandered back down the path and round into Dud's garden.

Nicky took the screwdriver and followed instructions. Then he lowered the hinged engine cover, was shown how to secure it, and afterwards helped Mr Dudzinski ease his work-gloves off. Although he was being as careful as he could, Nicky couldn't avoid dragging two of the dressings off with the right hand glove. He looked at the raw flesh on the tips. The yellow ointment his mum had applied made the burns look even more disgusting and painful. 'Shall I get my mum to come and sort out your plasters for you?' said Nicky.

'Mmm, better not,' said Mr Dudzinski regretfully. 'I don't think she'd approve of me working on the car in this state, somehow. Thing is, though, I got all impatient. I was dying to get the timing just right so I could take the car out for a run this weekend. Got a rally in Presteigne next week – that's in Wales. So everything's got to be right. Should be spot on now, I think. Pity I can't turn her over and have a listen, but that really needs a turn of the starting handle – to get the oil circulating properly. Still, never mind. Maybe you could help me push her back into the garage, eh?'

'Would you like me to turn the starting handle?' asked Nicky.

'Well, that'd be great, but I think it'd be a bit too much for you, Nicky, to be honest. Once the compression builds up, it takes a hell of a swing, you know. That's a big engine you've got to turn over.'

'I'll have a go,' said Nicky. He made his way to the front of the wonderful machine and got a grip on the starting handle with both hands.

'Tuck your thumb well in, just in case you do move it and it kicks back,' warned Mr Dudzinski. 'Set it in the down position and pull it up to twelve o'clock.' Nicky heaved with all his might but he could barely move it.

'Listen, leave it. Honestly, you'll strain yourself, leave it,' called Mr Dudzinski from the driver's seat.

'Shove up a bit,' whispered Oliver, and Nicky felt himself shoulder-to-shoulder with his invisible companion.

'Come on, you Unvisibles! A-one, a-two, a-three!' breathed Oliver.

'Mind she doesn't kick!' yelled Mr Dudzinski, sensing that Nicky was determined to put some beef into it.

With four hands gripping it tight (thumbs tucked well in), round went the starting handle with a fine sweeping motion. The engine caught and growled triumphantly. Almost instantaneously, though, the engine seemed to catch, the handle swung back violently, and both boys went sprawling in a heap.

'Fantastic!' shouted Mr Dudzinski. 'You OK, Nicky? I never thought you'd manage it! But wow, that was a near thing. A kick like that can break your arm!'

Nicky picked himself up and brushed the gravel off his palms. 'Hey, you're obviously tougher than you look!' laughed Mr Dudzinski. 'Tell you what, if you fancy a spin next week some time, once my hands are up to it, just let me know, eh? Maybe you could – you know – bring your mum. Only if she wants to, mind,' he added quickly.

'Well, I'm not sure. Maybe. Thanks anyway, Mr Dudzinski.'

'I keep telling you. Call me Steff. Or Dud if you like. Most people do.'

Nicky waved and left his neighbour to manoeuvre the rumbling car back into the garage and turned into his own gate, which he *tap, tap, tapped*.

'He's great, in he?' Oliver said. 'Fantastic car, eh?' He couldn't understand why Nicky hadn't jumped at Mr Dudzinski's offer of a ride for him and his mum.

'They've been out a couple of times,' said Nicky in a

low voice. 'They went out on his motorbike once. I'm not sure what went wrong, but I think something did. Anyway, Mum doesn't want to talk to me about it, and she only speaks to him if she has to.'

'Weird, aren't they, grown-ups?' mused Oliver.

17. At Nicky's

'Is that you, love?' came his mum's voice as Nicky opened his front door and let Oliver into the house.

'Hello, Mum,' called Nicky. 'Where are you?'

'I'm upstairs, getting changed.'

Round he went, three times, then he reached out and found Oliver's arm. He thrust the bag into his hand. 'Quick, get rid of this!' he said.

'Where?' Oliver sounded panicky.

'In there, the drawing room, where the piano is,' said Nicky. Then he had a sudden horrible thought. 'And then you come back here, OK? Don't go . . . sneaking about upstairs . . . spying. Right?'

'OK, keep your hair on!' said Oliver. 'What do you take me for? Flippin' 'eck!'

Mum's footsteps could be heard as she crossed to her bedroom door. 'Robbie and Riley will be here at seven, Nick. I was hoping you'd give me a hand with the supper. You're terribly late. What happened? I was worried about you.'

'I was chasing a ball and I slipped over on some grass,' Nicky lied. 'Had a nose bleed, so I had to wait in the First Aid Room for a bit.'

Footsteps bumped downstairs. Sally Chew appeared, buttoning up the sleeves of her silk blouse and looking anxious. She examined her son's face closely, satisfied herself that there was no major damage and bent to brush at the grassy stains on his knees. Then she put her arms round him and gave him a cuddle, starting to give his nose clusters of little light kisses. She was surprised to feel him squirming away. 'I'd better get changed, eh, Mum?' Nicky said. He could sense that Oliver had returned and he didn't want him seeing this or he'd never live it down.

He went quickly up to his bedroom and, once he sensed that Oliver was in, closed the door. He expected Oliver to take the mickey out of him for being a mummy's boy but that wasn't what was on Oliver's mind.

'Fantastic house, innit?' There was real admiration in his voice. 'All neat . . . and smart. It's like a show house or somethin'. All white everywhere, and clean. And all them books and classical CDs you've got! And I never knew you had a grand piano! Hey, where's your telly?'

'Downstairs,' said Nicky, taking off his uniform jacket and tie. 'Now I want to put my jeans on. Don't look.'

'Oh, come off it!' said Oliver, indignantly.

'Sorry,' muttered Nicky. 'It's just . . . it makes me feel weird . . . knowing you're there but not being able to see you.'

'Yeah yeah,' said Oliver. 'But how come you haven't got your own telly in your room? Or a computer? Your mum's not hard up, is she?'

'She thinks that bedrooms are for sleeping in,' Nicky replied. 'Not for working or watching TV. If we want to watch television, we use the drawing room and if we want to work, we've both got studies. Mine's in the next room. That's where I keep my PC and my books and everything. I suggest you sleep on the sofa in there. I'll give you a blanket.'

'Wow,' muttered Oliver. 'Must be great, having all this space to yourself. No wonder you do all right at school. My house is a right mess.'

'I thought it was great,' said Nicky. 'You're lucky, having all those magazines and comics. And it looks really . . . you know . . . lived in. It must be interesting, having a dad and a sister and juke box and everything.'

'Yeah, well, never get any peace, mate,' said Oliver. 'And me sister's a right old cow!'

'I thought she was OK,' said Nicky.

'You what? She's a psycho!'

Nicky's mum called out, reminding him that he was doing the *dauphinois* potatoes.

'The who?' whispered Oliver.

'Oh, it's just a way of doing potatoes – sliced, in layers, with cream and onions and cheese on top.'

'You do *cooking*?'

'One or two things, yes . . .'

'Flippin' 'eck!'

'Look, I've got to go. You'd better keep out of the way up here. I'll bring you up something to eat later. It's going to be bad enough being nice all through supper to people I can't stand, without worrying about you creeping about and bumping into things.'

'OK, OK . . . but wait! Is there a phone in your study?'

'Yes, why?'

'I've gotta call Carrie and tell her I'm staying over.

That's what you said, remember? There's no way I can use my mobile – I can't see where all the numbers are on it.'

'Oh yes, OK. Just keep your voice down. See you later.'

'Joke, yeah?'

'Oh, you know what I mean.' Nicky dashed to the top of the stairs, slapped the banister three times and ran down.

18. A Couple of Lucky Breaks

Robbie and Riley arrived in a lilac-coloured Daewoo hatchback. Nicky felt that was bad enough but they also turned up in matching *suits*. Robbie Williams had a bunch of flowers big enough to stand in front of a pulpit and Riley was carrying an old-fashioned leather music case, the type with the metal bar that goes over the handle, and a box of chocolates.

'Something smells really delicious,' grinned Robbie. 'Allow me.' He kissed Sally Chew on both cheeks.

'Goodness! You're so formal!' she laughed.

'The French way,' explained Robbie, bowing low. He presented her with the bouquet and then he presented Riley. Riley presented the chocolates, shook hands with Nicky's mum, then with Nicky. Formalities over, he felt ready to announce in a confident voice that he had brought his music. For later.

'Ready then, Riley?' said Robbie, and the two visitors put their arms round each other's waists, bent over and started banging their feet up and down on the spot. 'Scrum down, lads! Bind, bind!' yelled Robbie and they bundled Nicky and his mum through the door and into the hall, shouting, 'Heave!'

'Well done, well done! Good effort, you two!' puffed

Robbie, giving the rather startled Chews encouraging little mock punches on the arm.

'Can you sight-read music?' Riley challenged Nicky. And before Nicky had decided how to answer this one, Riley announced that he was a brilliant sight-reader. For his age. 'Aren't I, Dad?'

'You are extremely talented! Not only are you a first-class sight-reader, but you have a wonderful voice, especially for light opera,' beamed Robbie Williams. He turned to Nicky and his mum. 'Pollen alert!' he warned loudly. Nicky's mum, still clutching the enormous bunch of flowers, jumped several inches in the air. Recovering quickly, and dabbing at the orange stains on her white silk blouse, she allowed Robbie to take them from her and arrange them expertly in her largest vase. He set the vase up on a low table in the drawing room where he announced that the flowers provided just the right gala touch to the musical event they'd be enjoying after dinner.

'I don't believe in false modesty or beating about the bush, you see, Sally,' he went on. 'I'm a great one for directness and encouragement, aren't I, Rye?'

'Yes, Dad!' chimed Riley.

'Partnership and respect – that's how Riley and I get on.'

'Respect, man!' chirped Riley and raised his hand for a snappy high-five.

'Oh no,' muttered Nicky, cringing. He looked at his mum to see if he could make out what she was thinking but she had made herself busy, serving drinks and nibbles.

The longer the dinner went on, the more Nicky worried. *Dink dink dink* went his knife on the side of his plate. He was scared that Oliver would go to the lavatory and pull the chain, or even be tempted to creep downstairs to see what was going on. Knowing Oliver, he'd do something stupid and make a complete mess of everything. But the worst thing of all for Nicky was the way Robbie Williams kept slipping in stuff about partnership and sharing. For example, he paid mum a nice compliment about the *dauphinois* potatoes. Then, when he found out they were Nicky's speciality, he congratulated him, and asked Sally for her thoughts on positive parenting.

'Oh, Nicky's the one who looks after *me*,' smiled Sally Chew. 'And he's such a sensitive boy, I never have to force him to do anything, do I, Nicky?'

Nicky squirmed in his seat, not liking to be in the limelight.

'Do you and Nicholas like talking man-to-man?' Riley chipped in.

'Well, not *exactly* man-to-man, naturally,' laughed Sally. 'But we talk . . . yes.'

Normally, Nicky was perfectly happy with the amount of talking they did together, but just at this moment he wished they could take some time out to discuss this Robbie and Riley thing.

When the pudding turned up, Robbie suddenly became very serious, very solemn, very damp about the forehead. He blotted his shining, eager face with his napkin. 'Riley and I sometimes feel that there are certain things that boys want to say to each other that they can't really say to a woman. Don't we, Rye?'

'Yep.'

'Have you ever felt that way at all, Nicky?' he asked, trying to make it sound casual.

Nicky could see the tension in his mum's face. He suddenly realized that this was one of those 'life-changing moments' they'd been discussing in PSRE. Until Oliver came to him for help, he had felt that they were things that happened to other people, but suddenly here he was, face to face with another one. Would it break his mother's heart if he said what he truly felt? Because what he truly felt was that if he was expected to have Robbie Williams as a stepfather, and if he had to be partners with Riley as a stepbrother, and share his mother with both of them, then he would go crazy, or maybe just die.

'Shall we have a look at your music, Riley?' he tried to say. It didn't quite come out like that, but Riley got the idea and rushed for his leather music case.

'I would like to perform a short selection from *The Mikado*,' he called in a bold voice like a small vicar. His father's solemn look melted into one of adoration mixed with pride.

'Shall we make our way to the Music Room?' he joked, and held out his arm so that he could walk Sally through to the drawing room and a sofa that was facing the piano.

Nicky spread the music out in front of him with three sweeps of his hand as he settled on the piano stool, while Riley, backing into the curve of the piano like a professional, clasped his hands over his navel, spread his elbows and started to breathe deeply through his nose. 'I shall begin with "A Wand'ring Minstrel I"!' he declared, adding, 'Page fourteen, page fourteen!' He obviously felt that Nicky was slow finding it.

At that moment, something stung Riley's ear. It felt just as if somebody had flicked it with his fingernail. Ping. He gave a little squeak of pain. Up went his hand and down went his head. Nicky was too engrossed in the unfamiliar notes to notice. If he had, he would have been very worried indeed.

'All set, Rye?' said Robbie, winking at Riley. 'Come on, now! Posture, posture.'

Ping. 'Ouch!'

'Nice and still now, Riley. Relax. And big breath. And give it the Pavarotti treatment . . . !'

Nicky furrowed his brow and started to play the introduction. He did pretty well, considering he'd never seen this music before in his life. Robbie turned to Sally and told her loudly with another wink (ignoring the cleverness of the piano part) that when Pavarotti sang, he could make the chandeliers shake, and when he hit a certain high note, he could shatter a glass.

For a nine year old, Riley had a heck of a loud voice.

'A wand'ring MIN-strel I . . . !' he bellowed. As he hit the high note on 'min', the picture of Grandma and Grandpa, that normally sat accusingly in its silver frame on top of the piano, decided to fly into the air and smash into a table lamp.

There was a stunned silence.

'Good Lord!' gasped Robbie Williams, the first person to be able to speak. 'Careful, son. Step away from the piano a little. You must have given a little twitch.'

'I didn't do anything. It was him!' sulked Riley, pointing an accusing finger at the pianist.

Sally was quick to calm things down. 'I'm sure it wasn't anyone's fault. It was just a little accident. Never mind. These things happen. Now, Riley, how about trying another piece for us? What would you like Nicky to play?'

It didn't take long to clear the worst of the splinters of broken glass and to soothe Riley's wounded pride. He asked for a Coca Cola in a beer glass, had a good long swig, had his tears dabbed away and prepared for his big number. '"The Drinking Song" from *The Student Prince*,' he announced. He raised the beer glass and checked behind him to make sure he wasn't touching the piano this time. Then he told Nicky what page the song was on.

This time everything went without a hitch. Riley stood boldly and sang boldly and swung his glass boldly. Then they got to the chorus:

'Drink! Drink! Let the toast start!

May young hearts never part!

Drink! Drink! Drink!

Let every true lover salute his!

Sweet . . . HEARRRRRRT!'

Suddenly Riley seemed to lose control of his limbs, like a drunk. He came staggering towards his father, eyes wild, shouting 'Leggo! Stop pushing me!' As his father rose to stop him he got half a pint of Coca Cola chucked in his face. Then Riley gave a howl, his arm came up like a robot's and he suddenly lobbed the pint glass at the vase of flowers. The noise of the impact was spectacular and so was the flight of the flowers. They spread around the room like a sunburst.

'Riley!' roared Robbie. No doubt it was the shock that made him do it. But there was no talking through this little problem. Riley received a sudden and almighty SMACK round the back of the head from his dad.

Nicky, his fingers frozen to the keys in the shape of the last chord he had played, had mixed feelings. He didn't approve of violence, but at the same time, he was flooded with relief and gratitude. Because he knew, even before little Riley started screaming his head off, that that 'smack' brought down the curtain on positive parenting for him, and that the perfect partnership between Robbie and Riley Williams was not the only one that had suffered a serious setback.

An invisible hand squeezed Nicky's neck, the way a friend squeezes your neck sometimes, twice and, after a pause, three times.

'Thanks, Oliver,' he whispered. 'You just saved my life.'

19. Not Much Sleep

Lying in bed that night, Nicky stared at the shadowy ceiling. His mind was full of broken glass and flying flowers and snapshots of faces frozen at the moment of the smack. In the face of the fake Robbie Williams he read shame and defeat. Riley's face was distorted with outrage, injury, disbelief and terror. His mum's face was harder to read. He could see that she was bewildered and astonished – disappointed, certainly – but there was something else, too. She was good at disguising her feelings, and for a long time after the Williamses had left, never to return, she'd solved things for herself by getting busy with the mess in the drawing room while he loaded the dishwasher. After that, she excused herself and went out briefly, to check on Mr Dudzinski's dressings, she said.

But when she'd returned and said goodnight, she'd held him very tightly and said she was sorry for what she'd put him through and that it wouldn't happen again. He only realized how upset and guilty she was when he felt her tears plopping into his hair. 'I honestly didn't realize he was such a *creep* . . .' she whispered. 'Thank goodness we found out in time, eh? I'm sorry. I just wanted us all to be happy.'

Maybe he dozed a little, because he suddenly startled himself awake and lay on his back, rigid and panting. He strained his ears, thinking he heard his mum crying. No. Maybe not. Just a high whistling, like a radio signal. Then he definitely heard a sound. A creak it was. A floorboard on the landing outside. He waited, not breathing, all his senses straining. He knew almost by instinct that Oliver was in the room before he could actually hear his shuddering intake of breath.

'What's the matter, Oliver?' he whispered, sitting up and blinking three times.

'I dunno . . .' he stammered, his voice breaking. 'It's just that this invisible thing is dangerous, yeah? I mean, little things like going downstairs – it's really hard when you can't see your feet. And I tried to look at myself in the mirror just now. I tell you, if you can't see yourself, only your breath on the glass, it's sort of like you're not real – like you're dead. And I keep thinkin' . . . s'pose I cut myself. I could bleed to death and nobody would ever know what happened to me. Mum and Dad would just probably think I'd run away for ever because I can't concentrate and I'm rubbish at everything in school . . .' He couldn't speak for a moment but finally he managed to blurt out, 'I'm getting really scared, Nick . . .'

'Where are you?' whispered Nicky. 'Come over here. Sit down.' He patted the bed, *pat, pat, pat*. He felt it shift and sag as Oliver perched on the edge of it. He reached out in the darkness and found his trembling shoulder. 'Don't worry. You're not dead, you're real. And everything's going to be all right. I'll go with you and help you get the magazine back tomorrow, then you can say the words and get back to normal.'

Oliver seemed to take comfort from this but then

another wave of panic took him. 'Nicky. Listen to me. I've got to get some money. You've got to help me rob a bank or something! Not for me. It's for my dad!'

'What do you mean?' said Nicky.

Oliver sniffed. 'Because if my dad doesn't get some money soon, he's gonna have to close the shop down. He's owes people money. He's skint!' A paper tissue extracted itself from the box on the bedside table, scrunched itself up in midair, parped and flew into the waste paper bin.

'Listen,' said Nicky. 'For a start you're not crap in everything. French, maybe, but I can help you with that if you like. OK, you do muck around a lot . . .'

'Yeah, well, it's only to stop people taking the mick. Like Grover, Wilding the Head, Purvis – they all hate me. They're always going on about my stupid name, my ears, my teeth, my ginger hair – all that . . .'

'Look,' said Nicky. 'Calm down, OK? Let's think about this stuff one thing at a time. Nobody *hates* you, right? They just get a bit fed up with you clowning around, pulling faces, calling out, all that kind of thing. I know I do. And listen, you said you had to get your mind really focused to make yourself invisible. Am I right? Well that proves you must be able to concentrate when you want to!'

'Yeah, I s'pose . . .'

'So stop worrying, and get some sleep, OK? I mean, I think you're a good bloke, because if it hadn't been for you, Grover would have bashed my head in. And I hate to think what would have happened to me and Mum if you hadn't seen off those two tonight. So I owe you one.

But listen, you start robbing stuff and we're both going to end up in jail, OK?'

Oliver took a deep ragged breath and seemed steadier, more collected. 'Yeah. Well, you're right, I s'pose. But it would be handy if we could pinch those boxes back off Reggie Smarmface, wouldn't it? That wouldn't be like stealing, just getting our own stuff back. And that might make my dad pleased with me for a change, anyway.'

'Well, let's get the magazine first, find the words, sort you out – and worry about the boxes after that.'

Oliver agreed that that was a good idea. 'Hey, but how're we gonna get to Stourley? You got any money? I mean, I'll pay you back . . .'

'I've got about fifteen pounds,' said Nicky. 'And I don't want to ask Mum for more or she'll start asking awkward questions. Tell you what. Why don't we go by bike, and maybe bring them back on the train from Eastminster? That's only a couple of miles from Stourley.'

'Good one! But we'll have to go dead early or people will be like "Wow! A bike with no rider!" Have you got two bikes, though?'

'Yes. I've still got my old one in the garage. It's not quite full size and it's only got five gears, but that should be all right, shouldn't it?'

All this was a load off Oliver's mind. He thanked Nicky and told him that he was going back to the study to get a bit of sleep, they had a big day ahead. The bed wobbled as he stood up. He started to move away but halfway across the room, he hesitated. 'You were awake when I came in, weren't you?'

'Yes.'

'Worried about your mum?'

Nicky nodded. 'She thinks maybe it's unhealthy, not having a man around, for me as well as her.' Click went his nervous fingers, three times.

'Ah – she'll be all right! She's bound to meet some nice bloke you'll both like. I mean, she's brilliant, and she's dead pretty, int she?'

'Thanks,' said Nicky, not for the first time that night.

20. A Bicycle Not Made For Two

Nicky's mum was a little surprised to hear at 7.30 in the morning that Nicky was going round to a see a friend who was interested in buying his old bike, but she was secretly delighted to hear him use the word 'friend'. In her darkest moments in the night, she had cringed to think of the sheer awfulness of the relationship into which she had *almost* plunged herself and Nicky. That ridiculous man and that mad little Riley. And smacking him like that, after all his talk about equal partnerships and positive parenting. The most unbelievable thing about it was that it was all part of a cunning plan of Robbie's to persuade her to let him stay the night — because, in clearing up the drawing room, she had uncovered Riley's overnight things in a supermarket bag. The nerve of that man!

At her lowest ebb in the small dark hours, she had despaired of ever seeing her solitary son being 'taken out of himself', that mysterious condition that she felt was vital to his happiness. Now here he was, apparently doing it himself by going over to a friend's. Luckily, she had no idea that Nicky's 'friend' was Oliver Gasper from next door. If she had done, she would have had a fit.

★

Nicky wheeled both bikes up the pavement of Barnes Avenue. That was only common sense. As they got to the top and into Tarrant Way, however, Oliver convinced him that it would be OK for him to get into the saddle now, there being very little traffic about. After all, they had a fair way to go and they had better get moving. Nicky swung his leg over the crossbar and lowered himself on to the saddle, once, twice, three times.

Nicky found it fascinating to watch the other bicycle propel itself, especially when it swung itself round potholes or bumped itself up and down kerbs. It was a bit unnerving to ride directly behind it because he had no idea what it was going to do next, when it was going to brake, which way it was going to turn. Since he happened to know there was some idiot riding it, of course, he could take that into account and keep alert. But the drivers of several speeding white vans, whose minds hadn't adjusted to the possibility that they had just overtaken an invisible kid, didn't have the advantage of a rational explanation for the boy riding behind a riderless machine.

When Oliver had almost caused two crashes, Nicky had to take him in hand. He came up with a simple plan. At the first hint of an approaching vehicle or person, Oliver was supposed to move inside Nicky so that Nicky could grasp the handlebar of Oliver's bike and make it look as if he was simply steering it along. This idea worked brilliantly. It got them out of Marlbrook and into the country lanes beyond the Sandwich road without causing much comment, though it did provoke one or two early risers to call after Nicky that he wanted to watch himself, that was dangerous, that was. A passing paperboy called out, 'Yah! You flash idiot!' Nicky thought that was fair enough but Oliver was not so forgiving and told the paperboy exactly where he could go and deliver his papers. He was a big kid, and they had to put a heck of a spurt on to leave him behind.

By nine o'clock, they had covered eight or nine kilometres. The sun was shining, there wasn't a cloud in the sky, the breeze was behind them and the lanes were clear. Two lines of poplars that ran together into a V ahead of them down a slight incline meant that they could coast along and take a well-earned breather.

'How're you doing?' called Nicky, as Oliver's bike shot ahead and wobbled from side to side. Oliver was obviously standing on the pedals. *Ting, ting, ting* went Nicky on his bell.

'This is miles too small for me!' yelled Oliver. 'Talk about making your legs ache! The gears are useless – and my bum's getting sore.'

'Apart from that, great though, isn't it?' shouted Nicky, getting his head down and pushing hard after him.

'Fantastic, mate!' laughed Oliver. 'Waaahoooo!'

They stopped at the tiny village of Sharping and Nicky bought three items each – two Mars bars, two chocolate bars and two bottles of Coke from a dark little paper shop. The round-shouldered shopkeeper in the droopy cardigan looked a little surprised at the quantity his visitor had bought for himself but said nothing. As he turned to ping the till, two Bounty bars silently took off and hovered like little blue space capsules beside Nicky. He shoved Oliver aside by barging his invisible shoulder with his own, and grabbed the Bounties just as the shop-keeper turned round. 'Sorry, I'll have these as well, please,' he said and got a 'Kids today!' look. When they got outside, they had a row that started in whispers and turned into something louder as they got well up a country lane again.

'It'd be so easy!' Oliver said. 'I could just walk off with loads of stuff – sweets, drinks, cash, anything I fancied.'

'We've been over this,' puffed Nicky. 'It'd be different if you were on your own and starving so it was a matter of life or death. But you're not and it isn't. You've got me and I've got money. And that way nobody gets hurt.'

They pulled over by a gate into a field, leaned their bikes against the hedge, sat down in the warm grass and enjoyed their honest snack.

'Could be a matter of life and death,' grumbled Oliver juicily through a Bounty bar. 'Nah, you're right. I hate thievin' really. But it seems a real shame not to, you know, take advantage, like, while nobody can see me.'

'Don't worry about taking advantage,' said Nicky. 'When we get to the antiques shop, you'll have plenty of chances for that.'

Fired up by chocolate and sugary drink, the boys got cracking again and put another five or six kilometres behind them before they encountered anybody else. This was a very ancient, very slow and apparently short-sighted lady who wobbled on a bike out of a track leading to a farm without even realizing that anyone was coming down the lane. Nicky gave her a ding-ding-ding with his bell as they came up behind her – just a friendly warning – and she went into serious wobble mode. She obviously couldn't steer a straight course and look behind her at the same time. She clung grimly to her handlebars and swung towards the middle of the lane. 'Watch it! Get over, keep away!' she snarled as Nicky overtook her, as if he were a marauding fighter pilot.

'Mind 'ow ya go, ducks!' called a riderless bike that whizzed past her on the inside.

'Oh my!' screamed the poor old thing, and into the hedge she went.

'She'll be fine, don't worry,' urged Oliver, putting Nicky's bike between his and the lady in the hedge, and standing on the pedals to get a speed up. Luckily, since she had been going so slowly, it was a wide, cushioning sort of hedge, and since she never for a second stopped shouting at him, Nicky decided that there was no harm done, and raced after Oliver.

They were just through Binley when Nicky glanced over his shoulder and saw the police car. Oliver was ahead of him, so he called to him to drop back quickly and come alongside. Oliver didn't need to be asked twice, and as the blue-and-white Volvo overtook, Nicky, blushing furiously, did his best to adopt the submissive, invisible shape he took on to avoid the gaze of teachers. He nodded, wished he were truly invisible and clung gamely to both handlebars, squeezing each three times.

The nearside electric window wound down. The blue light gave a flash or two, the siren gave a piercing, single *wheeep* and the policemen called, 'Pull over!'

The blood now drained from Nicky's face. In a flash, he saw himself handcuffed, cautioned, driven to the nearest police station, his mother weeping . . . The poor old lady in the hedge. She'd probably called the police with her dying breath!

The policeman, having parked on the grass verge, got out. He shook his head and said, 'I don't think so, do you?'

'Pardon?' said Nicky. And then, remembering something he'd seen on the telly, he added, 'Officer.'

'Where are you off to with that?' said the policeman.

'What, this? You mean the other bike?' said Nicky, unnecessarily. 'Oh, I'm . . . er . . .'

'. . . just deliverin' it,' Oliver whispered in his ear.

'Just delivering it . . .'

'Well now, that's very enterprising of you,' said the policeman, 'but it's also a very good way of getting yourself killed. Have you thought of that?'

'Yes, sir, sorry, sir,' said Oliver, who'd had plenty of practice at owning up. He said it out loud. It just came out.

The policeman did a double take. He looked at the second bike that was now lying on the grass behind where Nicky was standing astride the crossbar of his own, and then stared hard at Nicky. 'Are you a bit of a ventriloquist, lad?'

'Um,' said Nicky.

'Gottle of gear, gottle of gear,' said Oliver, helpfully.

'Hey, that's really good!' smiled the policeman. 'Give us another go. Try and get the B-sound right.'

Nicky stretched his mouth into a straight line and prayed that Oliver wouldn't overdo it.

The policeman marvelled as the second bike spoke, and kept flicking his eyes back to Nicky's stiff mouth.

'I wish I was a little bug!' said the bike. 'Bug. Buh-buh-bug!'

'Fantastic!' said the policeman. 'Go on!'

The bike hesitated and then blurted out:

'I wish I was a little bug
With whiskers on my tummy.
I'd crawl into a honeypot . . .'

'. . . and make my tummy gummy!' shouted the policeman, finishing the line and letting out a great bellyful of laughter. 'I haven't heard that one for years! Brilliant! And your lips didn't move at all, hardly. I've got to hand it to you, son, you've got a gift. But look, seriously, this other bike – you're only going to hurt yourself, dragging that across the countryside. Not to mention endangering other road-users – not that there's many about, I grant you. I tell you what. Tell me where you're taking it and I'll deliver it for you. How's that?'

'That's really kind of you, Officer, but . . .'

'Stapleton's the name, PC John Stapleton.'

'Thanks, Mr Stapleton, er . . . I'm just trying to think of the address . . . um . . .' Hand over eyes, pat forehead three times, pat, pat, pat.

'Reginald Pugh, Period Furniture, The Green, Stourley,' said the bike.

'I don't know how you do it!' laughed PC Stapleton. 'I really don't! You ought to be on telly, you.' He bundled the talking bike into the back of the Volvo. 'What about you, son, do you want a lift?'

'Um . . . no thanks, very kind of you,' said Nicky hastily before Oliver got too clever. 'I prefer to ride; it's not far. If you wouldn't mind just leaving the bike somewhere near Mr Pugh's shop, I'll take it in to him later.'

'Good luck to you, then. What's your name, by the way?'

Quick as a flash, Nicky said, 'Oliver. Oliver Gasper.' He stood smiling as Oliver's bike was loaded into the police car, and waved as it drew away.

'Yeah, well, thanks a bunch!' groaned Oliver as the police car turned the corner. 'Droppin' me in it!'

'Serves *you* right, you mean. You and your gummy tummy,' grinned Nicky, 'You nearly dropped *me* in it! Anyway, you're lucky because he thinks Oliver Gasper's brilliant.'

'Well now we're gonna have to walk,' groaned Oliver.

'We'll try two-up,' said Nicky. 'You pedal and steer; I'll sit on the saddle.'

'How come I do all the 'ard work!' said Oliver, indignantly.

'I'll take my turn when we get into the traffic again,' said Nicky. 'Because it's going to look a bit weird if people see me just sitting there, and the bike pedalling itself along. So let's go. And take it steady, don't kill us both.'

It took about ten goes and at least five minutes before they could get the hang of it without getting the giggles or losing their balance and floundering all over the grass verge. Eventually they built up a bit of momentum and made some progress. In fact, they were lucky enough not to see a soul until they were about half a kilometre out of Stourley and, when they did, he was in a field on a tractor, doing a bit of muck spreading. 'Look, no hands!' Nicky yelled to him, waving both of them in the air.

'Oy!' puffed Oliver. 'Behave yourself, you!'

21. All You Can Eat

PC Stapleton had delivered Nicky's old bike all right. The only trouble was, it wasn't outside Pugh's antique shop, but just *inside* and the Unvisibles arrived just in time to see through the open door that Reginald Pugh himself was slapping a sticky label on to the saddle with 'Bargain – £30' written on it.

Oliver started spluttering and swearing under his breath, so Nicky had to tell him to watch it. 'Yeah, well the rotten so-and-so!' hissed Oliver. 'What's he doing nickin' bikes?'

'Don't panic,' whispered Nicky. 'He's just winding you up. The policeman must have told him that he was delivering the bike for you, so he wants to see your face when you realize he's put the bike up for sale, that's all.'

'Don't you believe it,' came Oliver's voice in his ear. 'He's a right crook, he is.'

Not wanting to draw attention to himself, Nicky turned his back to the shop, told Oliver to come with him, and started walking to his right, pushing his bike along at a brisk pace. He crossed Piggy Lane, and as he checked for approaching cars, noticed a Jaguar with the number plate 'REG 1' parked outside the side entrance to the shop. There were no houses beyond, only green fields and hedges.

The Unvisibles soon decided that it wouldn't be a

good idea for Nicky to collect Oliver's bike straight away. That fact was, it was gone half past one now; their backsides were sore, their leg muscles were stiff, and they were both *starving*. The only place they could find to eat in the village was on the other side of the green from the antique shop, and unfortunately it looked rather posh and pricey. It was called The Carvery.

The boys stood hungrily outside and looked at the menu. 'How much you got? Surely you've got enough to get something,' said Oliver hungrily.

'Yes, but don't forget we said we'd take the train – unless you fancy riding all the way back by bike,' hissed Nicky. 'And we've got no idea how much a ticket's going to cost.'

'Not much more than a fiver, surely. You only need a single.'

'Plus two bikes.'

'Yeah. So you could go six or seven quid on a meal. There! Look!' Oliver couldn't point, so he got hold of Nicky's chin and steered it round until he was looking through the window at a chalkboard inside that read: *Roast lunch – all you can eat, plus a choice of puddings: £7.50*

Three wipes of his feet on the doormat, three pats of the open door and Nicky pushed into the warm, dim interior, rich with the Sunday-lunch smell of roast meat and potatoes. There weren't many customers this sunny Saturday lunchtime, only two or three couples and a small family group, the children eating the roast, the parents tucking into something leafy. All heads turned as Nicky pointed out to the waiter the little pew seat in an empty booth where he would like to sit. The waiter, balding, with a thick moustache, an unsmiling, dark-eyed, middle aged chap in a crisply starched white apron, stood back to let him by. Nicky had to pretend to be about to sit on the opposite side, so that he could pull out the chair and let Oliver in, and then to change his mind and take up the aisle seat.

'Special roast for you?' asked the waiter, staring. He had a foreign accent, just a slight one. If he was being welcoming, he didn't show it.

'Yes, please,' said Nicky.

'OK, you follow to the carvery, yes?'

Nicky signalled for Oliver to sit tight and followed the waiter to a counter at the top of the restaurant where joints of meat steamed and streamed with mouth-watering juices, and a dozen stainless-steel dishes were heaped with vegetables and salads. He said he was hungry and the waiter served him slices of pork, lamb and beef, mashed potatoes, parsnips, peas, baby carrots, sprouts and rich brown gravy. Nicky added three roast potatoes, for luck, arranging them into a sort of mini-pyramid.

Grasping the overloaded plate in both hands, and aware that most of the other customers were grinning at him, he made his way self-consciously down the aisle and was shocked to see, settling into his seat, a man, smartly dressed in a light summer suit with a waistcoat. He was spreading out his newspaper and making himself comfortable. He was a red-faced man, a man with bushy black eyebrows and a narrow nose. His thick dark hair was slicked back so that the lines made by his comb still shone like wet furrows in a ploughed field. His piggy eyes picked out Nicky, dismissed him as unimportant, and turned to the financial pages again at once, while he said in a plummy voice, 'Get me a drink, Carlo, would you? Make it a double.'

Nicky felt the waiter's strong hands on his shoulders and heard him say, 'Oh, good afternoon, Reggie!' before bending to his ear and steering him into a pew in the next booth with the words, 'You must sit at next table. Mr Pugh is a regular. He sits there always.'

Nicky sat where he was steered, shocked, his appetite gone. Oliver was trapped in the inside seat by that horrible looking man – Reginald Pugh himself!

But you don't trap a starving invisible kid for long. Nicky heard a kerfuffle behind him and a shout of astonishment as Reggie's *Mail on Saturday* was snatched out of his hands and scattered all over the restaurant. 'Close that door, Carlo, for God's sake! There's one hell of a draft in here!' he roared.

At the same time, Nicky heard the crash and tinkle of glass and falling cutlery as Oliver scrambled over Reggie's table. Another roar from Reggie, 'What the . . . !' and, 'Don' worry, no problem!' from Carlo who rushed over to close the door and clear the decks. A second later, Nicky felt the partition shake, the laces of a trainer against his ear, and then a foot on his shoulder, as Oliver dropped in next to him. 'That's him. Smarmface!' whispered Oliver.

'I know,' whispered Nicky. 'Now what?'

'Eat first, plans later,' urged Oliver, and a fork rose, speared a roast potato and posted it into a black hole. Nicky's appetite was immediately restored and he concentrated on the task of keeping up, forkful for fork-ful, with his busily munching neighbour.

Carlo was none too pleased to see Nicky back at the carvery for another plateful. 'You again, eh?' he snorted, glaring, adding loudly for the benefit of the other cus-tomers as he re-filled the plate, 'You go a liddle bit careful, eh?' He patted his broad belly through his apron. 'You gonna go bang, no?'

By pudding time, when Nicky ordered pie, ice cream, sticky toffee pudding and cheesecake, the waiter looked furious. He would no doubt have gone raving bonkers if Nicky hadn't blocked his view of two chocolate profiteroles that rose from their plate and had the cream sucked out of them, before they vanished in mid-air, leav-ing three little floating dabs of chocolate – the size of two fingerprints and a thumbprint. They disappeared one by one with a sort of sloshing sound, followed a moment later by an enormous serving-spoonful of trifle.

'Go and sit down, for goodness' sake, you greedy pig!' scolded Nicky as forcibly as he dared, and nudged him along from behind till they got back to their table.

Carlo's dark eyes followed Nicky all the way. Another waiter, one dedicated to the idea of pleasing his cus-tomers, might have been delighted by the exceptional appetite of this young person, but as he moved suddenly in his direction, his starched apron crackling, Nicky had a sinking feeling that this particular waiter was going to rip him out of his seat and throw him across the bound-ary road on to the village green. So, when Carlo hurried past him to talk to Reggie, he cringed, then breathed a sigh of relief.

Judging by his appetite, Oliver seemed unruffled by this little scare, but Nicky guessed as he watched the last of the cheesecake on his plate vanish, that *he* was the subject of the spluttering conversation that Carlo was now having behind him with Reggie. He went to the till and paid up as quickly as he could, leaving a fifty pence tip. 'Thanks, lovely, I was a bit peckish,' he murmured apologetically.

'You call that *peckish*?' said Carlo. 'But seriously, hey?' he added, and he looked serious. 'Go visit the doctor when you get home, yes? Because maybe a big worm inside, I think.'

'Thank you,' said Nicky and was very relieved to get out into the sunshine. He and Oliver hurried away across the green, the latter belching loudly enough to make Nicky feel, as he pushed his bike along, that behind the flowered curtains of every half-timbered house round the green at Stourley were eyes that were turned on him. Having to place himself in the full glare of every other customer's attention in the restaurant while he presented his plate over and over at the counter like some demented Oliver Twist was his idea of hell. So, not surprisingly, he lost his temper and told the belcher that he was a greedy pig and disgusting with it.

He braced himself for an attack, certain that he would get a smack round the head at the very least. Instead, he was surprised to get a quiet apology. 'Yeah, sorry, mate. I am a bit of a slob sometimes, in I? But what are you so uptight for? *I'm* the one in trouble here.'

'What do you mean, uptight?' murmured Nicky.

'Well, not wantin' anybody to take notice of you. And doing that three-thing.'

'I don't know what you're talking about.'

'Course you do. Tapping things three times, clicking your fingers three times, turning round three times before you went out your front door . . . You're always at it!'

Nicky blushed.

'What d'you do that for?' asked the now familiar voice, not nasty, just wanting to know.

'Oh . . . I can't really tell you . . . it's just . . . for luck I suppose.'

'Makes you feel safe, does it?' asked Oliver.

Nicky stopped. That was it exactly. He'd never thought about it before, but – come to think of it now, Oliver was dead right – it did make him feel safe.

'And I thought I was the one scared to death!' laughed Oliver. 'Sad pair, us two, eh?'

22. Boxes

They sat in the shade of a chestnut tree on a bench on the green, feeling more ready for action with plenty of food inside them. They were just far enough away from The Carvery for them to be able to see Reggie coming out without him seeing Nicky, and also to have a good view of Piggy Lane and the antiques shop on the corner of it.

They had a plan now. When Reggie opened up the shop, Oliver would go in first and case the joint.

Oliver was keen to have a good old rummage in the shop until he found his dad's boxes. The most important thing was to get hold of the old magazine and smuggle that out. He would do that first because once he got hold of the 'auspicious words' again, he could get back to normal. He felt that *maybe*, with a bit of practice at concentrating, he would be able to switch himself off and on like a light bulb. But even if he remained invisible, smuggling out the boxes themselves would obviously be much more tricky, because Reggie's desk commanded a view of the Piggy Lane entrance as well as the front door. That was where he would need Nicky to come in and distract him somehow.

The Unvisibles waited quite a while. Reggie must be having a good lunch, they thought. Table by table, the people in the restaurant spilled out into their cars and drove away round the green. The front door swung shut and the 'closed' sign went up behind the glass. Still no sign of Reggie. Then a van, a smart blue Fiat with The Carvery, Stourley Village painted on its side in gold lettering, came out of the service road by the restaurant and pulled up in front of the entrance door. Carlo was at the wheel. Reggie emerged from The Carvery, adjusting his tie. He closed the door and got into the passenger seat of the van.

'Oh no, he's goin' off somewhere!' groaned Oliver.

'A bit over dressed for a van, isn't he?' observed Nicky.

'Oh no, look! He's only going as far as the shop. I wonder what he's up to. Greasy great slug, too lazy to walk,' came Oliver's voice bitterly.

'Maybe he's had too much to drink,' suggested Nicky.

'I'll go and have a dekko,' said Oliver. 'They'll be gettin' out the van in a sec.'

'That's fine, but don't leave me hanging on too long out here,' warned Nicky.

'It shouldn't take me more than ten minutes to see what he's done with dad's things,' said Oliver. 'So if I'm not back by then, come and find me, OK?'

Nicky heard Oliver's footsteps drumming over the dry ground and he guessed he must have timed his moment to enter the shop carefully, slipping between the two men as Reggie held the door open for Carlo, who was now wearing the sort of short-sleeved sports shirt that showed off his gold chain and powerful arms. Without his starched apron on, he was bow-legged as a cowboy.

After eight minutes, Nicky was starting to get worried. Exactly ten minutes after Oliver had left him, he set off, his bike ticking beside him, across the grass towards the road that ran round the edge of the green. He didn't steer straight for the shop but, remembering what he had once read in a history book about Julius Caesar performing 'a flanking manoeuvre', to get round his enemy, he veered towards the road a good fifty paces to the left of the junction with Piggy Lane. He was beginning to surprise himself; he hadn't realized before that you could be scared and enjoy yourself at the same time.

The Fiat van was still parked right outside Reginald Pugh, Period Furniture. Nicky wheeled the bike a little way down Piggy Lane and leaned it against the side wall of the shop, just in front of REG 1. Then, as he eased his way quietly round the corner, he was just in time to see Carlo, arm muscles bulging under the pressure of three obviously heavy boxes all wrapped in brown paper, came out of the shop. His short legs bowed almost into an O as he struggled across the broad, flag-stoned pavement towards the van. Reggie was strolling casually after him. His idea of hard work was to carry one small, flat, open box containing a number of items wrapped in newspaper. 'You'd better stow this towards the front, Carlo, stop it sliding about. This stuff is fragile and we don't want any breakages,' he said.

'Don't worry. I put behind others – very tight – can't move,' grunted Carlo.

Nicky took the opportunity to step unnoticed into the shop and to move quickly into the powerfully scented, rich, dark interior before either man noticed him. He had to squeeze past a dozen or more boxes and packages, all wrapped in brown paper, like the ones that Carlo was already loading. The bike had been moved into a further room. Quickly Nicky tiptoed along the rush matting pathway, over silky Persian rugs, under crystal chandeliers that tinkled as he hurried, past the ranks of polished oak tallboys and writing tables, corner cupboards and dressing tables, painted screens, gilt mirrors, wall clocks, grandfather clocks, embroidered Louis XV armchairs. Everything was glowing in light no brighter than candlelight, gleaming with beeswax, bright with Brasso, and smelling of money.

His heart pulsing, Nicky stopped by the desk where the computer was and stage-whispered, 'Oliver!'

He heard a bumping. Then a muted reply. He looked back. To his right, near the bike, a barred door led out into Piggy Lane. But to his left, just beyond the low beam where a swag of rich, embroidered material was artfully held aloft by loops of gold silk rope, was another door. This one was low, black and heavy. It was made of ancient oak and had a great brass lock. Nicky hurried across to it and placed his ear against the wood. A hefty thump shook the whole door and made Nicky jump back as if he'd had an electric shock but immediately he could make out, anxious and muffled, Oliver's urgent tones. He twisted the key in its lock, raised the latch, pulled the door open and peered into the gloom. He found himself looking down the steps into a vast cellar – though he didn't have an entirely unobstructed view, for hovering knee-high above the top step were two blue apple boxes, full of books and what Oliver had called 'odds and ends'.

'Whew! Well done, mate!' breathed Oliver's voice. Nicky lifted a finger to his lips and flapped at Oliver, warning him to back down a couple of steps while he pulled the door behind him. Carlo was coming in for another load. They held their breath. Thankfully, Carlo was too busy to look beyond the pile of boxes by the main entrance to the shop.

'I got a bit worried there for a minute!' whispered Oliver as the coast cleared. 'I couldn't start moving till they'd shifted a load of those boxes up the steps. Then they went and locked me in! Give us a hand with these quick – they're heavy!' Nicky stooped and took the top box as Oliver whispered, 'Help me get 'em outside.'

No sooner had Nicky got the side door open and bundled his apple box through to his invisible companion, than he had to close it again quickly. 'Off you go, quick, and stick the boxes behind the hedge!' he hissed.

Reggie and Carlo had finished loading and were heading in his direction! All Nicky could do was duck behind a tall bureau, start taking an exaggerated interest in the area that was devoted to eighteenth-century fire screens, and cross his fingers, one two three.

'OK, I make delivery to Louis's restaurant now,' he heard Carlo announce, even though he was still outside the front door. 'From here to Stanton Mellors is – what? – thirty minutes, maybe. Mind you, River Street can be busy . . . bad traffic. OK, so one hour there, one hour back – maximum. Then I drive back here, pick up a couple boxes of champagne for myself late this afternoon, yes?'

Reggie agreed with a grunt as he stepped into the shop and Carlo followed, clapping his shoulder loudly. Nicky realized that he could see them both now, in the distorted reflection of a convex mirror with golden plaster birds flying round its frame. He hoped (blink, blink, blink) they couldn't see him. 'Hey, and what sort of money are you looking for, for the cups and things you found for his missus?' Carlo was asking.

'Don't settle for anything under a hundred pounds,' said Reggie. 'He's been on at me to look out for 1930s china for her. She collects anything with a flower pattern, particularly if it's cream coloured rather than white. So I had my man Gasper pick up a nice little assortment of Titian Ware cups and saucers and plates for me at the Darnley House sale.'

You liar! thought Nicky. Lucky Oliver didn't hear you call his dad 'my man' or you'd be getting a kick where you weren't expecting it!

'Tell Louis they're getting damned hard to find,' Reggie was saying. 'Very collectable and all that . . .' Suddenly, Reginald Pugh's florid face turned even redder as he caught sight of Nicky. 'You! What are you doing in here?'

Carlo's moustache bristled as he formed his mouth into a grimace. 'Careful, Reggie. This kid have a big worm in his tummy. Maybe he eat the furniture, hey? Ha ha!'

'I'm . . . er, just looking,' said Nicky, as innocently as he could. 'It's . . .' he swept his arms around, '. . . it's lovely . . . all these fine . . . antique things.' He was floundering. 'How much is this?' he blurted out, dashing at the label dangling from a handsome cupboard-thing with shelves on top. Even as he did so, it flashed into his mind that this must be the Welsh dresser that Oliver's dad had sold to Reggie for . . . £850, was it? He flipped the label over and saw that the piece was now priced at £8,500! 'Ah!' he gasped, adding as a lame afterthought. 'I've only got about a fiver on me, I'm afraid.'

Reggie put his hands to his hips and scowled.

'Er . . . But mainly, I noticed you had my bike, so thank you very much!' gabbled Nicky, lifting it up and pointing it at the door.

Reggie wasn't having that. 'What do you think you're up to?' he bellowed.

'What?' said Nicky, taken aback by the violence of this outburst. Out of the corner of his eye, he saw the side door open a little. Oliver must have slipped back in.

'A policeman entrusted that bicycle to my safe keeping, and I have it on his authority that it belongs to a boy I happen to know,' drawled Reggie.

'Ah, well, yes, in a way . . .'

'A stupid annoying boy, as a matter of fact; a shifty, fidgeting boy with no manners who can hardly speak the Queen's English.'

Reggie's last remark must have struck Carlo rather painfully because he suddenly seemed to lose control of his temper, too. He thrust an accusing finger at Nicky. 'That make two annoying boys!'

Behind him, a grandfather clock shuddered and made a gonging sound. 'Look out, Carlo, you fool!' snapped

Reggie. 'Mind that clock!' Carlo froze. 'That's a George the Third Lancashire Longcase! The insurance alone nearly put me in the poorhouse!'

'But, Reggie, I didn't touch it . . .'

Reggie ignored him and turned to Nicky again. 'You don't happen to know him, do you?' he demanded. 'He's a ginger-haired little yob with ears sticking out like Dumbo the Elephant?'

'There's no need to be rude!' said Nicky bravely. 'He's a friend of mine.'

'I shall be as rude as I damn well like in my own damn shop, young man! But since you claim to be a friend of that idiot, take the bike! I shall be glad to see the back of it. And tell your brainless chum that I shall be giving his father a call on Monday to inform him that his son has been cautioned by the police for being a danger on a public road!'

'That will learn him!' agreed Carlo, a second before the George the Third Longcase clock arrived on his head like a felled tree. Its swan's neck pediment, its giltwood capitals and its gilded glass-decorations scattered themselves around the room.

'The clock struck one,' Nicky heard Oliver say quietly through gritted teeth as the booming noise faded and the astonished Carlo clutched his battered pate.

'You clumsy idiot!' screamed Reggie.

'Don't you shout to me I am clumsy idiot!' Carlo screamed back. 'Look what your elbow done!' A porcelain vase, tall, pink and beautifully decorated with cupids was rocking from side to side on top of the side table near Reggie's right elbow. With a shriek, he tried to steady it by diving sideways, a little like a rugby scrum half delivering the ball to his centre. As soon as his fingers came into contact with the precious and delicate thing, however, it danced over his hand. Astonished, Reggie tried to get both hands on it but it shot out of his grip like a bar of wet soap, bringing down a shower of chandelier crystals before smashing itself to pieces on his bended knee.

'Cuckoo!' said the pieces of the clock to the pieces of the vase, which was odd for a clock that had always chimed up to then.

'Well, if you'll excuse me,' said Nicky, getting a grip on the handlebars of the bike and steering it towards the Piggy Lane exit, 'I'll be on my way. Goodbye.'

He wasn't surprised to get no reply.

23. Not Much Time to Think

As soon as they hit Piggy Lane, the Unvisibles made a mad dash to get round the corner and out of sight behind the hedge – to give them a bit of breathing space – because breath was one thing that Oliver didn't seem to have much of. 'That paid him back . . . ! The lousy, stinking, swindling . . . !' He sounded terribly upset, his pain coming up in great sobs.

Nicky looked up and down the lane before opening the five-bar gate into a newly mown field. He watched the spare bike slide behind the hedge, pushed his own through and squatted down, feeling the sharp jab of holly or hawthorn in his back before he found a softer spot. 'You're all right now,' said Nicky. 'You're OK, just take it steady . . .'

'Taking the mickey . . . callin' me Dumbo the Elephant, saying I'm an idiot . . . trying to get my dad to have a go at me . . . !' It was still too much for him.

Nicky sensed that his friend was as much shocked by the scale of the damage he'd caused as hurt by Reggie's insults and threats. Being invisible didn't mean that you stopped finding out nasty things about yourself, he realized. If anything, it made things worse. For these reasons, he decided that now was not the moment to share his discovery that Reggie was selling the Welsh dresser for ten times what he'd paid for it or that he had taken some china out of the boxes that belonged to Oliver's dad. Instead, he felt for Oliver's invisible arm, just above the elbow and gave it a tap, just to let him know that he was there and it was OK by him if he was upset. 'What did you do with your dad's stuff, Olly?' he said quietly.

'I only had time to dump it behind the bogs round the back of the shop,' sniffed Oliver.

'We'd better fetch it here, then,' said Nicky. 'Hey, did you find that magazine while you were in the cellar?'

'No, I never got the chance to have a proper look,' said Oliver, taking a deep breath, 'What with them two wrappin' up bottles of champagne and shifting them up the stairs in crates. And all my dad's stuff was just tipped out on the floor. I s'pose Reggie must have started checking through it all to see if there was anything worth having. I just about had time to shove it all back in the boxes and try to get out the shop. Then I found out they'd locked the cellar door on me! So I was stuck till you came along.' He was calmer now and Nicky could hear him wiping at his nose with his sleeve. 'You wait here,' he said with a final sniff. 'I'll nip back to the bogs and get Dad's stuff. Reggie and his mate will be too busy clearin' up to be thinkin' about much else.'

'Will you be able to carry them both? They're quite heavy.'

'Yeah. It's not far.' He was away and back in a minute or two, just long enough for Nicky to give some thought to the stuff that Reggie and Carlo had loaded into

Carlo's van. What was an antiques dealer doing selling crates of champagne? And why would he bother to wrap them up, just to deliver them to a restaurant?

The arrival of two flying apple boxes interrupted him. Nicky opened the field-gate and let them float past. There was a grunt as Oliver dumped them on the grass, after which the Unvisibles settled to the task of turning everything out and looking at each item carefully. Mostly, they found books, all except the valuable one that Reggie must have taken out. There were one or two brass ornaments, a chocolate box containing a bunch of old postcards, some faded, framed photos of men in army uniform. There were magazines – several *National Geographics*, and some copies of *The Illustrated London News* – but there was no sign of the one Oliver was looking for.

While Oliver carried on flicking through them and shaking them out, Nicky's eye was taken by the two grimy little paintings that he found among the clutter. They were both about thirty centimetres long and fifteen centimetres high, that was all, and the figures weren't fully formed in either. In one, there was a red shape that Nicky thought might be a dog, lying in the bottom left hand corner of the picture. And there was another shape – a bonfire or maybe somebody curled up. In the other picture, Nicky was positive he could see a bicycle and two figures sitting quietly beside it, looking to the right. They were watching another figure, definitely a boy. He was standing up to his waist in water, calling out through his cupped hands.

The hair began to stir on the back of Nicky's neck.

He looked from one picture to the other and it was obvious that the setting was the same in both, though the angle was slightly different. Factory at the top, he noted. Bridge. Figures in the foreground on the left with some trees in the distance beyond them. River bank. And the river wasn't just blue, it occurred to him. He felt himself prickle as a wave of excitement raised gooseflesh on his arms and chest. Because, no, the river wasn't just blue – it was speckled with fat pink dots and white dots and grey dots. In fact, if you looked closely and ignored the dirt and the cobwebs, you could see that in both paintings some of the smaller spots of paint had become peaked and pointed like little bits of icing on a cake. So these were oil paintings, done on some kind of stiff board. And they looked remarkably like the one that he had so painstakingly begun to copy in Mr Stapleton's Art class: Seurat's picture, *Bathers at Asnieres*.

He heard Oliver throw down the copy of *National Geographic* that he had riffled through for the twentieth time and cry out in despair, 'It's gone! It's not there. He's probably sold it already, so I've had it! I'm gonna be stuck like this till I die!'

'Wait a minute, wait a minute!' said Nicky. 'We've got to think about this! Who would he have sold it to, eh? I mean, nobody's going to go into that fancy shop to buy tatty old magazines, are they? A posh *book*, yes, you can understand that.' He was thinking of the illustrated book translated by Baron Somebody. The one that Reggie had been very quick to pay Oliver's dad fifty pounds for, which meant it must be worth a lot more. Nicky hurried on, though, not wanting Oliver to be hurt any more than he was already. 'I know he's sold Carlo the china . . .'

'What china? Oh yeah – that china!' exclaimed Oliver as it dawned on him. Nicky could imagine his lively face lighting up. 'There were all those cups and saucers and jugs and dishes in there, weren't there! So he's sold 'em, has he? The rotten . . .'

Nicky slapped his forehead and started to let out a yell that he had to work hard to stifle. 'Hey! We're missing the point, Olly,' he said excitedly.

'What?'

'Here's a quiz question for you. What do people usually wrap up china in when they're moving it?'

'Newspaper,' sulked Oliver.

'And what might they use if they haven't got a newspaper handy . . . ?'

'Pages out of a magazine!'

The next move, as far as Oliver was concerned, was obvious. He had better get up the lane again and check out Carlo's van! He just hoped he hadn't left already.

'Wait, wait, wait! I'll come with you,' called Nicky.

They shoved Oliver's dad's stuff under the hedge, got through the wide gate and jumped on the bikes, ped-alling like mad and skid-stopping near where Reggie's Jag was parked. Nicky let Oliver do the reconnoitring and waited in the shadow of a cracked old brick buttress that supported the wall of the building. He heard loud accusing voices coming through the Piggy Lane entrance, which confirmed his guess that Reggie and Carlo were still in the shop, making sure they collected up all the bits of the clock and the vase, and having a bit of a row about who was clumsier.

A splashing of gravel and the thumping of feet nearby told him that Oliver was hurtling towards him. 'Carlo's leaving any second! I heard him say he's got to get started over to Louis's place in the next couple of minutes or he won't be back in time to open his own restaurant for business,' he panted. 'Quick, come and help me find that box of china!'

Nicky chased up the lane and round the corner. The back doors of the van weren't locked, luckily, so Nicky was able to peer in. He felt Oliver pushing up beside him. A wall of boxes covered in brown wrapping paper confronted them.

'Give me a hand to shift some of these,' urged Oliver. 'The china must be wedged behind them.' Brown paper ripped itself away from one of the boxes and Nicky saw it was crammed with bottles of champagne.

'What's an antiques dealer doing selling champagne?' said Nicky.

Suddenly, Reggie and Carlo's voices became alarmingly loud. 'Take this, quick!' snapped Oliver, ignoring Nicky's question. Nicky felt his wrist being grabbed roughly. Something with a little bit of weight to it was slapped into his hand, something plastic but with the smoothness of polished glass and metal there, too. 'It's my mobile,' whispered Oliver. 'I'll have to go with the van, nothing else I can do. Shut the doors behind me and get out of sight yourself – quick! Then you better call the police and tell them what's happened to me!'

24. Panic Stations

'Tell the police what, though?' Nicky said to himself, as he squatted behind the hedge again, sweating now with the effort of getting both bikes away and out of sight. Things were getting horribly out of control and he felt gripped by panic.

He ran his thumb over the invisible keypad, trying to visualize the layout. He didn't have a mobile himself; his mum was worried that the radiation might damage his brain. Still, he had a pretty good idea how they worked. He felt for the 'Clear' button and got a bleep out of it. It occurred to him that if somebody came now – the farmer, maybe – they would think he was stark staring bonkers – a boy sitting by himself in a field, staring at the palm of his hand! But he knew he mustn't think like that. There were things to do.

But what? The whole thing was turning into a nightmare. Supposing he managed to call the police. He ran the ridiculous conversation through in his head:

'*Hello, Police?*'

'*Can I help you?*'

'*Yes, my friend Oliver Gasper is trapped in a van.*'

'*I see, and whereabouts is he now, sir?*'

'*Um.*'

'*Can you describe your friend, sir?*'

'*Um.*'

No. Definitely no point in calling the police – and yet he had to do something! Oliver was in deep trouble. He must be scared to death, squashed in the back of that van, not sure where he was going, terrified that he might – literally – never be seen again.

And here he was, Nicky Chew, stuck with two bikes and two boxes full of stuff that belonged to somebody else. How was he ever going to get them home? How was *he* going to get home? His mum would start worrying soon. Maybe he should try to ring her . . . No, that would be too complicated. He leaned back and was almost relieved to feel the sharp stab of hawthorn or holly in his back again. It was a sharp reminder to think, and not let his thoughts charge about like headless chickens.

Strange, though, how even those thoughts that refuse to be ordered about can be useful sometimes. The crazy thought of chickens running about minus their heads triggered something in his memory like a clip from a video: of Mr Dudzinski doing his war dance round his back garden, screaming like a demented football fan and flapping his burned fingers.

Mr Dudzinski – and he had a car!

As anybody who has tried phoning Directory Enquiries on their mobile with their eyes closed knows – it's tough. And it's even tougher if you're not familiar with the layout of the keys. Nicky was a bright boy, though, and he was patient and pretty cool in this emergency. Somehow, after lots of agonizing false starts and several random connections that raised his hopes and dashed them again, he got through to the operator. He tried to persuade her to put him through but she said she couldn't and handed him over to a recorded voice that gave him the number he should ring. He had nothing to write it down with, but he held it in his memory. And for some lucky, wonderful, beautiful reason, Mr Dudzinski answered the phone straight away.

'Hi, it's me, Nicky.'

'Are you OK, Nicky? You sound a bit shaky.'

'Can you come and help me?'

'Course I can. What's the matter? Where are you?'

'You won't say anything to Mum, will you?'

'Not if you don't want me to. Where are you?'

Nicky told him and asked him to come in the car, not on the motorbike, because there were things that needed collecting.

'OK. Don't worry about a thing. Wait there. Give me your number. Ah, no, I've got it, it's come up on my screen. Sit tight and I'll be with you in about twenty-five minutes.'

Nicky slipped the invisible phone into his pocket. He was going to pat it three times to make sure it was there because it was invisible and if he dropped it he would almost certainly not be able to find it again . . .

But then he thought, No. Stop that. It was time he grew out of that three-thing.

25. The Chase is On!

The gunshot came twenty-four minutes and sixteen seconds later. BLAM! Nicky nearly jumped over the hedge with fright.

Then came another one, nearer this time, from up the lane near the green. He scrambled over the five-bar gate and looked left, straining his ears. He could hear a throaty rumbling roar. He gulped and drew in his breath – and a moment later he saw the sun glint on the great froggie eye of the left headlamp of a dark blue 1929 Lancia Lambda saloon as it swallowed the corner in a curving, elegant sweep and drew to a throbbing halt beside him.

'Sorry about the backfire!' yelled Mr Dudzinski, pushing his goggles up on to the top of his old-fashioned leather helmet with one hand and leaning out to crank up the massive handbrake with the other. 'Still haven't got the timing quite perfect. How are you, Nick?'

'Can you help me get these boxes into the back?' said Nicky and immediately remembered that Mr Dudzinski's gloved fingers must still be painfully tender. Mr Dudzinski wasn't in the least put off, though. There was easily enough room in the spacious rear area for a couple of boxes and a bike. The other one needed lashing to the running board, something he managed with hardly a wince. Then he said casually, rewinding his white scarf round his neck as he spoke, 'What's happened to the other guy? I presume there is another guy?'

'We've got to find him. He's in bad trouble,' said Nicky.

'Right, hop in the front. Where are we off to?' No awkward questions. No big deal.

'Stanton Mellors.'

'Over the other side of Canterbury?'

'I think so.'

'OK. Whereabouts in Stanton Mellors?'

'Do you know River Street? I think it's River Street.'

'That's the ghastly main street, I think. But there's a beautiful little cul-de-sac just off it that runs down to the river, I remember. There's a restaurant there – Louis's Bistro. I've eaten there a couple of times.'

'That's it!' yelled Nicky. 'Louis's Bistro – got to be!'

The small rutted track by the gate left little room in the narrow lane for backing up, so pointing the long chassis up towards the green with no power steering must have been something of a strain on Mr Dudzinski's sore fingers, but he didn't make a fuss. The car turned in the narrow lane on its own axis, like a black cub. Away they went with a bang and a rising series of growls.

When they hit the boundary road at the top of Piggy Lane, Reggie was standing on the corner. Maybe it was the backfiring that had alerted his attention to the car when it first came by or maybe it was pure chance. Either way, although Nicky tried to duck out of sight, he was too late.

'Hey! Hey you! I want a word with you, you damned little thief!'

'What did he say?' shouted Mr. Dudzinski.

'He's after me. Would you mind putting your foot down?'

'One of my favourite things!' grinned Mr Dudzinski. And VRRRRRRROOOOM, off they went.

With the engine roaring and the wind spilling under the tilted windscreen and whipping through his neat hair, Nicky was having the ride of his life. There was no safety belt and nothing much to hang on to, except for the arms of the wickerwork seats, but he felt completely safe in Mr Dudzinski's charred hands.

In ten minutes they were winding up the broad ribbon of Compton Hill, where the sun flickered through the canopy of the beech trees like strobe lighting, heading for Winsett and Thaddington. Then Nicky noticed that Mr Dudzinski's eyes were flicking more and more often towards his mirror.

'Know anybody who drives a Jag?' he yelled.

'Lose him!' screamed Nicky, feeling marvellously overexcited.

'Aggghhh!' screamed Mr Dudzinski, partly because of the strain it put on his sore fingers but more because he was enjoying himself hugely, and he threw the Lancia down a lane that popped up on the right. The tyres screamed gloriously and the back end swung out too far for a second so that it needed a tug back into line. Nicky turned his head and saw REG 1 fly past and up the hill, anchors on and sliding – but with far too much forward momentum to make the turn. He'd be backing up now, though, that was certain, so no time to relax.

Right again, again, left and into a single track lane, the banks lush and thick with vegetation and grass growing through the tarmac in the middle. It ran straight for quite a way – too far, really, if you were trying to keep out of sight of someone who was after you. Cow parsley came slapping at them and bunches of leaves from leaning hazel trees swooped down and made them duck. 'I have a hunch this comes out by the river at Pluck's Gutter!' yelled Mr Dudzinski. 'Let's hope we don't meet any farm traffic!'

'There he is,' warned Nicky as the dangerous, crouching shape of the Jaguar materialized behind them.

'I see him. Hold tight.'

With a double-pump of the clutch, a grinding rip as the gears grappled and meshed and a full throated growl as Mr Dudzinski's right foot mashed down on the throttle, the Lancia leaped forward. The windscreen bolts rattled and the back axle whined in triumph as they took the curve on what felt like two wheels, throwing up a trail of dust and weeds as they cut too close to the bank. A quick change down to take the first part of a tight double turn . . . Then they saw the tractor and trailer chugging towards them.

'Don't worry,' yelled Mr Dudzinski cheerfully as he pushed down hard, not on the brake but on the throttle. The tractor driver hadn't seen them yet. He was in the process of switching a cigarette from one side of his bottom lip to the other with his tongue. Suddenly he saw a low, dark, blue shape cut round him on the wrong side. It flew over the ditch to his left by his great rear wheel, through a gap in the hedge, banked in a spectacular arc along the side of a baked and ancient dung heap and leaped in a flurry of dust and flying flintstones through an open field gate and back on to the lane.

The tractor driver barely had time to shout at the rapidly disappearing madman, when the masterful blare of twin horns alerted him to the fact that he was on a collision course with another lunatic, only this one was going like the clappers in a Jaguar Mark 2.

'Waaaahooo!' said the occupants of the sports car, one of them for the first time in his life. Mr Dudzinski (a seasoned waaahoooer) was more or less right about where the lane came out, and after that they settled to the business of getting to Stanton Mellors while Nicky told Mr Dudzinski what had happened.

At first, he edited the story a bit, explaining only how he and his friend Oliver had gone to get back the stuff that Reginald Pugh had stolen from Oliver's dad and how Oliver had stowed away in Carlo's van so that he could recover a box of china that Reginald Pugh had given Carlo to sell to Louis. He told him how worried he was, about Oliver and about himself. Almost the hardest part was admitting how scared he was of getting into trouble, never having deliberately got himself into any before. Mr Dudzinski took this very much in his stride, but much as he liked him, and however warm and grateful he felt towards Mr Dudzinski for coming to his rescue with no questions asked, Nicky found it really hard to bring up the fact that . . . you couldn't actually *see* Oliver.

Still, Mr Dudzinski's way of listening appealed to Nicky a lot. He didn't ask any questions, hinting that he doubted Nicky's judgement or wondering whether he was right to go taking the law into his own hands by stealing Mr Gasper's boxes back. He wasn't a great one for 'Uh-huh' or 'Uh-uh'. He just made it clear, by the way he kept on driving and paying attention, that he trusted the boy to be doing the right and honourable thing and that he would stick by Nicky in pretty much the same way that Nicky was sticking by his friend Oliver.

So Nicky decided to tell him the whole unedited story, including all the stuff about Oliver being invisible. At the beginning – the part about the smell of Juicy Fruit, the Willybeast and the appearance of the words *Feed the fish* . . . *JBL* on the white board – Mr Dudzinski had to pull the car over and screech to a stop in a lay-by for a few seconds. 'Sorry,' he said, turning in his seat so that he could face Nicky. 'Sorry, but I just want to make sure I'm getting this straight.'

He got it straight, shook his head, blew a great breath that puffed out his cheeks, revved like mad and zoomed off again. Now that he was over the shock, he could hear the rest of the story and keep driving, occasionally muttering, 'Astonishing!' and 'Brilliant!'

Maybe it was because Nicky had told him things that he wouldn't have revealed to anybody else that Mr Dudzinski found the courage to tell Nicky something that was painful for him to talk about. He told him about what had gone wrong with Nicky's mum and him. He just came out with it, and Nicky did his best to make it easy for him to do so.

'I like your mum a lot,' Mr Dudzinski yelled over the

roar of the engine. 'She's . . . a nice woman and . . . she's lovely . . . Well, you'd know that, anyway. Anyway, soon after I moved in next door we started to hit it off, you know . . . just chatting over the fence, really. Recipes, we talked about. We talked a lot about cooking, funnily enough. And she started making jokes about me and the bike: boys and toys, stuff like that. And how I should be careful I didn't kill myself because she'd seen me come off once. It was embarrassing, nothing really dangerous, only I came round that sharp corner into Byron Road – the one where the traffic coming down has to go into it blind on the wrong side, because of the parked cars. I was going up, saw this car coming at me, couldn't brake in time. You just have to bail out when that sort of thing happens. All you can do is let the bike slide and make sure you haven't left your leg underneath.

'Anyway, she happened to be walking past. I felt . . . stupid. Just lying there in the road, bit bruised but perfectly OK. That's what your leathers are for, to take the sting out of that sort of thing. But I was annoyed because you know these bikes are built to crumple at various points. So there was a little bit of damage and I knew it would cost me. And I thought maybe she'd get all – you know – flustered and worried and maybe start ticking me off. But you know what she said to me?'

'What?' asked Nicky.

'She said, "I quite fancy a ride on that some time."'

'Mum said that?'

'That's exactly it. That's exactly what she said. I was surprised but I thought, right, you're on. Then I asked her out to dinner but I had a panic on at work that evening and, in my rush, I forgot the name of the restaurant at which I'd booked the table. Stupid, that was. That got us off on the wrong foot. But anyway, couple of weeks later . . . do you remember I did that risotto for you and her? Anyway, I told your mum I had two tickets for a concert at the Winter Gardens. Blues evening it was, plenty of good bands – I thought she might just be interested. The car went on the blink at the last moment but I remembered what your mum had said about fancying a go on the bike. Well, I had a spare helmet, so I asked her, was she kidding about fancying a ride or did she want to come? She said fine, why not?

'Anyway, on the day, on the evening – d'you remember? – I came round with the bunch of anemones for her? So we jump on the bike. It's a bit tricky for her, not having ridden pillion before, but it was fine. Off we go. She seemed a bit quiet but I knew she wasn't the chatty type, wouldn't want to shout over the engine. I took it pretty easy on the way there, didn't want to worry her, but she seemed well balanced, you know what I mean? So I opened up a bit on the way home. We had a great evening, nice concert, great meal. Came home – she was holding on to me – I thought, you know, this is it, she likes me! But the following day – nothing. Not a word. And she never spoke to me at all till the other day when I burned myself. She obviously thinks I'm a total idiot – Dud by name, Dud by nature.'

'No, she doesn't think that at all,' said Nicky.

'I thought about it afterwards, you know, a woman like her, attractive, sophisticated. I thought, Oh no . . .

she must have felt so *ridiculous* sitting on the back of a motorbike, too ridiculous even to talk about it . . .'

'I think you're wrong. It's just that she's a bit mixed up. I think you *should* talk about it,' Nicky said.

'Do you really? Do you think there's any point?'

'Definitely,' said Nicky. 'I think she's nervous about getting let down . . . She's been let down a lot. And she's nervous about me getting let down, too.'

'Oh, I see. You mean by getting mixed up with the wrong sort of bloke?'

'But you haven't, have you? Let *me* down, I mean.'

'Let's hope not, eh?' said Mr Dudzinski, clinging grimly to the big steering wheel and squeezing everything he could get out of the roaring, rattling old Lancia.

26. Reggie Makes a Splash

In spite of its nice name, Stanton Mellors was no beauty spot. They passed the old covered market hall, and that was the only attractive thing they passed. There was a boarded-up Plaza cinema, a Lo-Cost supermarket and a grimy and grafitti-covered row of shops in Station Road. When they followed the one-way system into River Street, the traffic hit a bottleneck and slowed to a choking crawl in the heat. One or two curious passers-by, dressed for the summer in traditional English Lycra T-shirts and stretch shorts, their white middles squeezed into rings like Michelin men, shouted questions. They were the kind of questions that owners of vintage cars always get asked: 'How old, mate?', 'What make?', 'How much?' Still, they made Mr Dudzinski stop worrying about Nicky's mum for a bit, and they made Nicky very nervous about how long they were taking to get to Oliver.

It was a blessed relief to get away from the noise and the smell of traffic and into the quiet, tree-lined spur road, left past the Oxfam shop. Almost immediately, Mr Dudzinski pulled the car over to the right and parked in the shade of a lilac tree dripping with fragrant cones of blossom. He took off his leather helmet and goggles and

157

ran his hand over his mad hair. He made a little face at Nicky followed by a couple of pointing gestures with his head to indicate that they should get out here and take a look.

Some of River Street's ugly properties had rather surprisingly well-kept gardens that dropped down in a series of terraces, stopping at a low boundary wall, low enough to sit on and look across the road at the river beyond the railings. Nicky stepped up on to it. Four men in a boat on the far side of the river slid across the surface like a silent insect, and away towards Canterbury. Otherwise, there was nothing on the river except some ducks and a pair of bobbing coots. He edged along the wall until he saw through the gaps in a thick fuchsia bush, Carlo's Fiat van, parked not twenty-five metres away, directly alongside a canopy with *Louis's Bistro* announced on it. The bistro was the only building in the cul-de-sac, apart from the run-down boatyard beyond with its steep slipway down to the water.

Carlo, a pink Elastoplast X on his battered bald spot, had his back to him. He was sitting at one of several silver tables under the canopy, drinking coffee with another man, who was very heavy, his moon face bordered by cropped black hair. He was wearing chequered cooks' trousers and a vest. There was nobody else around. Nicky tugged at Mr Dudzinski's sleeve to indicate that it was fine for him to take a peek since the two men were obviously engrossed in conversation. Mr Dudzinski looked and told him, yes, he recognized the big man in the chequered pants; it was Louis. 'They're only open for dinner,' Mr Dudzinski whispered, which explained why there were no customers about.

Suddenly, Louis laughed, stretched, stood up, strode over to the van, threw the back doors open and stepped back, hands on his hips, to look at the cargo. As Carlo rose to join him, Nicky ducked back out of sight while Mr Dudzinski took out his mobile and moved into Nicky's old spot, pretending to be deep in a murmured telephone conversation.

'Yup. Carlo's got the doors open . . . No sign of your friend Oliver, not surprisingly . . . And Louis has gone over to look at the boxes. You said there's champagne in them, didn't you?'

'Yes,' whispered Nicky. 'Carlo's selling them for Reggie.'

'Aha! A little bit of smuggling, eh? He buys the champagne miles cheaper because it's tax free in France and sells it over here illegally for a huge profit. Hang on . . . Yep. Lots of waving now. They're pulling some of the boxes out, piling them in the road behind the van. Carlo's crawling in . . . he's backing out. He's dragging something – another box, only a different sort.'

'Is it an apple box?' asked Nicky.

'Yes, that's it, an apple box. Now Louis's having a poke about in it. He's taking something out. Unwrapping it. Looks like a cup. He's smiling. He likes it, nodding away. He's taken the box and put it down on the table. He's turned to help Carlo. Carlo's picked up two crates of champagne now. He's heading for the café and . . . Wow!'

Nicky heard an almighty crash followed by angry bellowing. 'What's happened?'

'He was just walking along – then all of a sudden, he sort of chucked the lot into the road! There's champagne running everywhere! Louis is bending down to pick up one of the unbroken bottles . . . Now *he's* dropped it! He's straightened up. Now he's jumping up and down and he's . . .'

'Rubbing his backside?' put in Nicky, hopefully.

'Exactly! How'd you know that?' said Mr Dudzinski, spinning round to look at him directly.

'I told you about the kick-up-the-bum manoeuvre for creating confusion among the enemy. That's one of Oliver's favourites. What's happening now?'

'It's incredible!' said Mr Dudzinski, having a good look and not bothering any longer with the pretend mobile conversation. 'They're having a punch-up! One minute they're having a laugh over a nice cup of coffee. Next minute, they're knocking six bells out of each other. Quite handy, being invisible, eh?'

At that moment, a Mark 2 Jaguar with considerable damage to its front bumper, radiator grill and headlights pulled up sharply alongside Mr Dudzinski and Nicky. The driver's window rolled down and out came Reggie Pugh's very red face, and his blazered arm pointed a terrifyingly solid-looking revolver right at the pair of them.

'Listen to me, you two! I used this weapon in the army, and I swear to you, after the day I've had, I'm in just the mood to use it again right now. Give me back my property you damned thieves. You've taken some stuff from my cellar. I want it back.'

'Hey, steady on! He's only a kid, you know. You can't go waving guns at—'

'Shut up!'

Mr Dudzinski did shut up, which meant that Reggie couldn't fail to hear the sounds of breaking glass and a violent quarrel coming from down by the Bistro. He waved Mr Dudzinski and Nicky forward with the gun and herded them down the slope towards the punch-up. 'Stop that, you idiots!' he yelled. 'What the hell is going on here? Are you out of your minds? Don't you realize that that champagne is worth three hundred pounds per dozen!'

Carlo and Louis staggered apart, panting and bruised and torn. 'He kick my bottoms!' wailed Carlo.

'Rubbish! I not touch. Only when he say to me I am fat froggy!' accused Louis.

'Big liar! I don't speak these things.'

'Shut up!' commanded Reggie. 'Shut up and listen to me.' Champagne was streaming over his shoes into the gutter and running down the boatyard slipway into the river.

They noticed the gun then and were immediately silent. Carlo and Louis were standing by the van and Mr Dudzinski and Nicky were now by the tables in front of the bistro.

Oliver's familiar voice whispered in Nicky's ear. 'Am I glad to see you! Stand in front of the box of china so Reggie can't see it.'

Nicky pretended to stagger, raised his hands in apology to Reggie and moved between him and the box on the table. He heard paper rustling behind his back and prayed that Reggie, standing in the middle of the road, was too far away to notice. He needn't have worried. The power of having a lethal weapon in his hand had gone to Reggie's head.

'You two,' he barked, meaning the gaping Carlo and Louis. 'Get the rest of those boxes inside and clear up this mess. I have some business to settle with these other gentlemen.'

Carlo and Louis settled to their given task like zombies. Reggie grunted triumphantly, then waved the revolver to his right.

'You!' he barked at Mr Dudzinski. 'Get the things this boy stole from me out of your Tin Lizzie and put them on the back seat of my Jag. It's unlocked. And . . .' (He was beginning to think of himself as a bit cool now, a bit of a gangster.) '. . . don't try any funny stuff or you'll make things very unpleasant for the kid. Do you understand?'

'Don't worry, Nicky. He won't hurt you,' said Mr Dudzinski with a reassuring wink, and he made his way slowly up the road towards the cars. The Jag was still double-parked next to the Lancia on the slope where Reggie had first pointed the revolver at them.

The rustling of paper behind Nicky became more urgent.

'Now, just so that we understand each other,' said Reggie to Nicky. 'I shan't be pressing charges, even though I am perfectly entitled to—'

'I don't think you're entitled to threaten people with guns,' piped up Nicky, partly to cover up the rustling behind him; it was getting rather frantic.

'Keep quiet!' warned Reggie. 'I shall tell you when I

want to hear from you. Meanwhile, try to get this into your thieving little head. If you mention any of this to anyone – he waved the revolver vaguely in the direction of the unloading operation that Louis and Carlo were silently carrying out – I shall report you to the police and bring charges against you for theft—'

'Found it!' whispered Oliver. 'I've got the page with the words on. I'm stickin' it in your back pocket. Hang on to it whatever you do. I won't be a sec. There's something I need to do.' Nicky felt a folded paper being stuffed into his pocket as promised, and a pat on his back, then two more.

'—and I shall have that man arrested as an accessory,' droned Reggie, pointing at Mr Dudzinski. 'And as for that stupid friend of yours . . . What's his name? – Oliver Gasper – I shall have him too, because I know damned well he's mixed up with you in this somehow.'

Under Reggie's orders, Mr Dudzinski now picked up both the apple boxes. He was making his way round to the offside passenger door of Reggie's car with them, when the driver's door suddenly flew open by itself and slammed shut. The Jag began to roll forward, gathering speed as it freewheeled down the slope, straight at Reggie. He saw it coming and shouted to Louis and Carlo, 'My car! It's slipped off the brake! Stop it for God's sake, before it . . .'

Louis and Carlo had no intention of trying to stop a ton of tempered steel and glass that was charging straight at them. Yelling, they threw themselves sideways, scattering tables and chairs while the Jag ripped off one of the doors of the Fiat, before spinning sideways and sending Reggie into a screaming dive right over the railings and into the river.

What with all the dashing to and fro, the scramble for the lifebelt from its post by the boathouse, the worry about whether the Jag would slide all the way down the slipway, and the rest of the general mayhem, Nicky was completely unaware of the piece of paper being tugged out of his back pocket. That was why he was so shocked when he turned to look behind him and saw . . . the ghost of Oliver! He was standing, grinning toothily at him, like a boy-size X-ray, only in colour. No, he was more like one of the plastic specimens of animals in the Bio Lab, with all bones and folded innards showing. Mercifully, he only stayed like that for a few seconds. Then he was his normal, opaque, solid self, holding a sheet of crumpled yellowing paper in one hand and a revolver in the other.

'It's not a real gun – it's just a fake!' laughed Oliver.

A little distance away, Major Reginald Pugh his hair smeared over his gasping fishy face like stringy weed, was being dragged roughly on to the bank by Carlo and Louis while Mr Dudzinski called the police.

'Just like Reggie, then,' grinned Nicky. 'Nice to see you again, by the way.'

27. Home Sweet Home

There was a lot of grinning on the drive back to Marlbrook.

There was a fair bit of – 'You all right, mate?' 'Yeah, I'm all right!'

There was plenty of – 'Did you see the way the Jag went wheeeeee . . . smash!!' and 'What about that fat bloke when I booted him . . . ?' and 'What about when Reggie got that *gun* out?'

Mr Dudzinski was particularly delighted that his ancient Lancia had proved itself a winner against a much younger Jag. He was very taken by the idea that the Jag's brakes might have let it down when it came up against the tractor – though it might have been Reggie's driving, of course.

Oliver got on with Mr Dudzinski like a house on fire from the word go, and immediately took him up on his invitation to call him Dud. Nicky said no, if they weren't going to call him Mr Dudzinski, they were going to call him Stefan, not Dud; he wasn't a dud. So Stefan it was, and Stefan was fascinated by the whole process by which Oliver had made himself invisible. 'It must have taken an amazing amount of concentration!' he said, with real admiration.

'Yeah, come to think of it, I s'pose it did,' admitted Oliver. 'I surprised myself there. But I doubt if I could do it again. I'd keep remembering how scary it feels and get all distracted.'

'I bet you could,' put in Nicky. 'Because you had some good laughs, too, didn't you?'

'Well, yeah! Hey, you won't say anything, will you, Stefan? I'd rather keep it a secret.'

'I promise I won't say a word, not if you don't want me to,' Mr Dudzinski replied solemnly.

As the Lancia rumbled closer to Shelley Road, the mood started to change. 'You don't reckon Reggie'll come after us, do you, Stefan?' said Oliver, gloomily. 'He knows where I live, yeah? And he's going to be pretty mad about having this stuff nicked back off him.' He patted the apple boxes he was sharing the back seat with.

'Don't worry about it,' Mr Dudzinski reassured him. 'He knows we've got enough on him to put him inside for a fair old time. He had no business to be threatening us with a gun, for a start. Fake or not, there's a law against that.'

'And the smuggling,' added Nicky.

'Smuggling?' exclaimed Oliver.

'Champagne,' said Nicky. 'The stuff you smashed into in Reggie's Jag.'

'Nicky told me Reggie was keen on taking regular trips to France,' said Mr Dudzinski. 'He wasn't just buying antique furniture. He must have been buying the champagne tax free and bringing vanloads through customs, claiming it was for his personal use, then selling it on illegally for a fat profit.'

'He'd just come back from France when we delivered the dresser!' Oliver remembered. 'He was bragging to my dad that he went there all the time!'

'Was he? There you are then! So well done, lads! You've put the stoppers on a racket that could easily have gone on for years without anyone being any the wiser! Because I can't imagine those three are going to be on speaking terms after what happened today, can you? Especially when it comes to working out who's going to pay for all the damage.'

It was after six when Mr Dudzinski dropped them off outside Oliver's. They'd unloaded the bikes and the boxes, thanked one another and said what a great time they'd had for the umpteenth time. The Lancia was in gear and ready to pull away, when Nicky called out, 'Stefan!'

'What's up, Nick?'

'Are you doing anything tomorrow?'

'What's tomorrow – Sunday? No, I don't think so. Why?'

'You don't fancy a trip up to London, do you?'

'What with you two – in this? What are you, gluttons for punishment?'

'Us, and Mum, maybe.'

'Oh, well, yes, that'd be great, but I don't think she's going to want to come, somehow.'

'I'm pretty sure she will,' said Nicky, though actually he was just hoping.

'Have you got anywhere particular in mind?'

'I've got to check something, then I'll let you know exactly where by tomorrow.'

'OK. See you then.'

'See you, Stefan,' said the Unvisibles.

28. Birthday Girl

A change had come over Carrie Gasper. Oliver could sense that something had happened to her as soon as he and Nicky slipped through the front door and heard the beat – not of one of her usual wild tunes, the sort to hang on to the mantelpiece and headbang to – No, this was something mellower, something to sit down and tap your foot to, and it was insinuating itself in gentle waves of pleasure throughout the house.

'What's that?' mouthed Nicky, his head going gently up and down.

'The Ink Spots. "Java Jive", one of Dad's favourites,' explained Oliver, his face taking on a ridiculously ecstatic look and letting his body turn to bouncing, spongy rubber. Together the pair of them umcha-ed into the sitting room where they found Oliver's sister sitting in the big armchair, legs stretched out, gazing at her left hand that swayed to the music at the end of her outstretched arm, while her right hand reached into a family-size packet of salt and vinegar crisps.

She screamed when she caught sight of them, but just a normal squeaky little *you-made-me-jump* scream, not her usual *right-you're-gonna-get-your-head-smacked* number. 'Where you been?' she said, spraying them with a salt and vinegar shower.

'Muckin' about with Nicky,' said Oliver evasively, adding, 'Give us a crisp.'

'I know you been round Nicky's,' she said, getting up and sliding an arm round Nicky's shoulder and holding the packet under his nose with the other hand. 'We met yesterday, didn't we, darlin'?'

'Uh-huh,' said Nicky, shyly taking a crisp. Oliver plunged his hand in and came up with a great wodge of them, all of which he managed to get into his mouth at once.

'And it's a jolly good thing we met, too. Because if you hadn't come over to invite Oliver to stay over with you, I would never've gone down the Arts Centre with Charlie. And if I hadn't gone down the Arts Centre with Charlie last night, he might never have given me this.' She held her left hand in front of his face. Next to the eyeball ring on her pinkie, wound round the significant third finger, was an even more enormous piece of jewellery, featuring two carved silver skulls kissing.

'It's lovely,' Nicky said. 'Congratulations.'

'Ooh, THANK you . . . !' she said and gave him a smacking kiss that made his ear whistle. 'What you starin' at?' she snapped straight afterwards, turning on Oliver in a tone that hinted at more familiar, more dangerous Carrie – but she was only kidding, apparently.

'We went and got your dad's stuff back from Reggie Pugh,' said Nicky brightly, just to keep things sweet.

'Did you now!' she said, wide eyed. 'What, just went over there and said, "Give us back my dad's stuff!" and he give it you?'

'More or less,' said Oliver.

'No, come on, what'd you do? You didn't go and nick it back, did you?'

'Put it this way,' said Oliver. 'He knows we've taken it back, and the police are talking to him right now, but he's not gonna do a thing about it.'

'I dunno what you're on about, but Dad's gonna be well chuffed about that! I mean, it's not just the money, it's the principle of the thing, innit, Nicky?'

'Absolutely. It's the principle of the thing. Although, a little bit of money might come in handy just at the moment . . .'

'Brrrmm, brmmm, not half!' went Carrie, hanging on to an imaginary steering wheel and singing *Happy Birthday to Me*. Then, just as a little warning to Oliver that she could still do a bit of stirring, she said, 'Oh, by the way, there's a letter come today with your school crest on the envelope. You ain't been a naughty little boy again, have yah?'

The blood drained out of Oliver's already pale face and a tell-tale look of dread took control of it. 'You're kiddin'! You're winding me up,' he said, but she strolled over to the mantelpiece and picked up an envelope, waving it by her ear with her finger and thumb as though it might speak its awful news to her.

'Ah, let's just chuck it!' said Oliver, without much hope.

'I don't think so, Oliver. Remember how upset Mum and Dad were when you hid your half term report?' sang Carrie. 'They'll only find out and you'll be even deeper in the doo-doo, won't you? No, I think we'd better just keep it for them to read when they come back, yeah?'

There was just enough of her killer look in her eye to prevent Oliver making a fight of it.

'It's probably nothing. Don't worry about it,' said Nicky, as convincingly as he could. 'Is there somewhere we get on line for a minute? Do you mind?'

'What for?'

'Just a bit of research.'

'Ooh,' said Carrie, impressed. 'Is this for the Ghandi project you two are working on?'

Oliver looked blank and Nicky grabbed him by the shoulders and steered him out of the room before he complicated things. Oliver led the way up to his room with all the enthusiasm of the condemned man ordering his last breakfast, cleared a space round the computer and switched it on.

The first thing Nicky wanted to look up on the Internet was 'Georges Seurat'. They found hundreds of websites — but it wasn't a problem to sift out the information he was looking for: that *Bathers at Asnieres* is in the National Gallery collection in Trafalgar Square in London.

'That's it! That's where we're going tomorrow,' said Nicky. 'Trafalgar Square. And don't forget to bring those two little pictures out of the odds and ends box.'

'What for?' said Oliver.

'Just a hunch,' said Nicky. 'But if I'm right, you're going to be *well* pleased.'

'OK then, I'll go as long as they've got a McDonalds there,' groaned Oliver. 'You finished with this?' He nodded at the screen, and when Nicky got up out of the driving seat, sat down in it and said, 'Right. I just want to check out www.periofurn.co.uk. Then we'll go round your house.'

Reginald Pugh's website was everything you'd expect of somebody running a smart antique furniture business, with loads of JPEGS of the 'many, fully authenticated quality pieces' that could be shipped 'with total peace of mind' to any part of the world. And then, right at the end, under 'Special Offers' there was a mugshot of Reggie himself. 'Look at him,' snarled Oliver, 'smiling his fat head off.'

'Well, at least he won't be including champagne among his special offers from now on,' said Nicky. 'And I have a hunch he won't be ripping off your dad again.'

'You bet, buster!' said Oliver, putting on an American advert voice. 'Attention crooks and criminal organizations everywhere! Straighten up right now, or you are going to have to deal with . . .' He waited for Nicky to join in the chorus.

'. . . The Unvisibles!'

During dinner, Nicky was trying to think of a way of gently persuading his mum to take a trip to London with Mr Dudzinski without stirring up muddy waters. He prepared the ground by explaining how Stefan had driven all the way over to Stourley to pick up him and Oliver and their bikes when they got stranded. That deserved one or two Brownie points, surely.

'Fancy cycling all that way!' she said, missing the point. 'And Oliver's miles too big for that old bike of yours! You must have been exhausted.'

'Knackered,' agreed Oliver.

Not the sort of language she felt comfortable with, but she ignored it. Although she'd been quite shocked at first to hear that Nicky's new friend was Oliver Gasper, she was delighted that Nicky enjoyed his company enough to spend a whole day with him, and equally pleased that he had volunteered to have him stay over. She was learning that when you got to know Oliver, he was good-hearted, fun to have around, and doing his best to behave. She also sensed that he'd been more or less struck dumb from the moment he entered her house. Deep down inside her a question was forming about whether the house wasn't rather too spotless and ordered – from a boy's point of view.

Her suspicion that he was a bit rough round the edges was confirmed by the way he tackled his supper, which happened to be spaghetti, but she quickly forgave him for getting sauce stains round his ears when he cheerfully told her he'd only had spaghetti out of a tin before, and that *that* was the kind you can write your name with. He'd never had broad beans either, apparently, or leeks – but he was willing to have a go at them, and she admired his pluck, and launched into a confession that her mother used to force her to eat marrow that made her sick by not letting her have any pudding till she'd cleared her plate.

Things loosened up after this confession and Oliver felt confident enough to ask her a question. He said, 'Do you mind if I ask you something, Mrs Chew?'

She said no, thinking it would probably be a question about vegetables. But Oliver wasn't one for pussy-footing about. He wanted to know if she thought Mr Dudzinski was an idiot.

He came right out with it. She wasn't quite ready for that one, and she answered, blushing hotly, that she wouldn't have put it that way, no, not at all. She thought he was a very nice man.

'Because he really likes you, you know, doesn't he, Nicky?'

'He . . . he does,' faltered Nicky. This wasn't his sort of territory, but now that Oliver had brought things out into the open, he found the courage to push on. 'He told me. He thinks you're lovely.'

'What! He said that to you . . . about me? What on earth made him say that? I mean, I've hardly spoken to the man lately.'

'We were having a man-to-man chat,' Nicky explained.

'Oh, man-to-man, was it? I see. What else did he say, then?'

She listened carefully to Nicky's report, nodded and looked thoughtful. Finally she said, 'I'm the one who's been an idiot, aren't I?'

So the National Gallery was mentioned, and the proposed trip to the National Gallery in Mr Dudzinski's Lancia.

'It's a fantastic ride,' enthused Nicky. 'And maybe you could help out with some of the driving – you know, in case his hands get sore.'

That was that; she said she'd go next door and discuss the trip with Mr Dudzinski right after supper.

29 - Completing the Picture

Nicky and Oliver raced up the steps of the National Gallery and stood panting next to a Japanese family of six who were taking it in turns to take photos of one another against the background of Trafalgar Square. Oliver's eyes were taken by the sudden waves of startled pigeons, the kid screaming to be looked at from the back of one of the lions, the paddlers in the fountains and the birds sitting on Nelson's head.

Oliver laughed and interrupted Nicky to point out all the bird poop to him. Nicky was trying to get his bearings. He recognized South Africa House and the church of St Martin-in-the-Fields. Charing Cross station must be over behind there; that was where he'd arrived once before when he came on a primary school trip. Leicester Square was somewhere behind. He turned to look in the direction taken by his mum and Mr Dudzinski – Stefan – a minute or two before.

Nicky had tried to indicate to her on the journey up to London, without being rude, that there was something special that he and Oliver wanted to see *by themselves* in the National Gallery. His mum had been a bit uncertain about letting the boys go wandering about in a strange place in a big city. Luckily, Stefan had quickly rescued the situation by telling her that they'd be fine and that he wouldn't mind having a quick tour of the National Portrait Gallery which was next door. Mum agreed to go with him but insisted that they were to meet up in half an hour, right on the steps where they were standing now; that was the deal.

The lady at the enquiry desk told the boys exactly where *Bathers at Asnieres* was hanging. Up they dashed to the first gallery on the right and hurried through the second set of double doors.

'Look at that!' said Oliver as they were engulfed in refreshingly cool, conditioned air. Nicky turned to see Henri Rousseau's famous painting of a funny-looking tiger crouching in the rain in a jungle that looked as though it had sprung from overheated pot plants. 'We've got that one on our calendar!' said Oliver.

'And that one's in the art room at school!' said Nicky, pointing out Van Gogh's yellow kitchen chair. They recognized some of the others, too, from Mr Tennyson's books, including the Cézanne that Oliver thought was rubbish, but they couldn't see the painting Nicky was after – until they had pressed straight ahead into the adjoining room.

Nicky didn't need to point it out. *Bathers at Asnieres* was enormous, bigger by far than anything else in the room, astonishingly big, marvellously bright. It dwarfed the boys as they stood looking up at it.

'Look at the size of that! You couldn't even get that in my *room*!' exclaimed Oliver. And then, turning to his friend, 'Seurat, Sewer Rat – it's him, isn't it – the dotty bloke old Stapleton was ravin' about! Wow!'

'And look at these!' said Nicky, shrieking with excitement – and he wasn't a boy who made a habit of shrieking in public. He had caught sight of eight relatively tiny, relatively drab little efforts, gathered into bunches of four on the wall to the left of *Bathers at Asnieres*.

He and Oliver stood shoulder to shoulder while Nicky read out the notice for the sketch numbered 1283: 'One of thirteen oil on panel sketches for *Bathers at Asnieres – 1883–4,*' it said. The sketch was called *Clothes on the Grass, 1883* and that's exactly what it was – a shapeless bunch of clothes lying on a riverbank. There was a sketch with the same background called *The Rainbow*, one called *Scene at Asnieres*. 'Look,' whispered Nicky, because the attendant was watching them warily now. 'Look at the water – green dots, pink dots, blue dots – you can see he's put those ones on sideways. And look, he's done downward dots for the green grass on the riverbank. Quick, let's have a look at your dad's pictures.'

Oliver swung his back to Nicky so that he could take them out of his little rucksack for him. Then they held one each. They looked at them together. Then they looked at the ones on the wall.

'Same size,' whispered Oliver.

'Exactly,' said Nicky.

They compared the scenes – the riverbank and the river were in all of them, the factory and the bridge in most. They looked at the figures, the colours. One or two of the sketches on the wall were signed on the bottom left hand side, but not all. So that meant that even if

Oliver's dad's weren't signed, they could still be . . . well couldn't they be?

'Must be!' breathed Nicky, his eyes widening.

'Got to be, mate!' grinned Oliver, his whole face lit up with amazement and pleasure. True, there was a bike in one of Mr Gasper's pictures – and not in any of the ones on the wall. Nor were there any sketches of a red dog.

'But look there!' said Oliver, and pointed back to Seurat's massive painting. There was a red spaniel, in the bottom left hand corner, large as – larger than – life. 'That's him!' spluttered Oliver, jabbing his finger at the indistinct red form on the picture in his hand. He looked at the sketch Nicky was holding – the one with the bicycle – and they both searched the walls for one like it, but without any luck.

'Come over here, Oliver,' said Nicky and he tugged him by the sleeve towards the other bunch of four sketches. They turned out to be studies for a picture they didn't have in the National Gallery. The notice explained that the actual painting was in Chicago and it was called *La Grande Jatte*. Again Nicky read out the note: '*This may have been executed in the studio, as Seurat, studying earlier sketches, began to experiment with his composition and the placement of figures in it.*'

'Now! Do you see? Your dad's pictures are experiments! Seurat was trying to decide what to put in his final painting of *Bathers at Asnieres*! He left out the bike but he stuck in the spaniel – see? It says he did thirteen sketches. These two could *easily* be two of them – or maybe ones nobody even knows about yet!'

There wasn't much else to say. But Oliver said it anyway – jumping up and down at the same time –
'We're RICH!'

30. The Theme From Star Wars

After the experts were called in and consulted and had provided their favourable reports; after the trips to the auction houses, Christie's and Sotheby's, and what with the press interest, it turned out that the sketches were worth a lot of money. A *lot* of money, thousands and thousands of pounds, in fact! There was easily enough money to pay off Mr Gasper's debts, refurbish the shop, buy a bigger van, provide a family holiday to Disneyland in America and take Nicky along as well.

Not to mention the new Nissan Micra for a very happily engaged, tattooed birthday girl, who now referred to herself as a 'recovering Goth'.

And what about the dreaded letter from school that Mr Gasper ripped open on the Monday morning after his return from Ireland? It was just after he had learned the astonishingly good news about the likely value of the odds and ends that his son and his new friend had recovered for him, so there was a shadow of a smile on his face. Oliver braced himself for a tirade, expecting the smile to be wiped off any second.

He needn't have fretted because the envelope contained no complaint about absence or poor behaviour, only the school newsletter with a notice in the STOP PRESS column:

Parents will be saddened to hear that, as a result of problems of a personal nature, Mr P.F. Purvis MA (Oxon), Head of Modern Languages, has tendered his resignation, with immediate effect. The Headmaster has reluctantly accepted his resignation and has invited Mr J.L. Lever BA (Hons), to assume his duties until a permanent replacement can be appointed.

'Oh, what a shame,' sighed Oliver's mum. 'Such a lovely man, too. Charming on Parents' Evenings, he was! I wonder what sort of problems he's been having.'

How wrong can you get? thought Oliver, but he kept his thought to himself and tried not to grin triumphantly about what his pranks with Madamoiselle Fifi had led to. He hardly dared believe his luck, so he certainly didn't want to push it.

How did Mr Dudzinski and Nicky's mum get on? Blissfully happily. Now that they'd had a good chat and each was much clearer about the way the other was *really* feeling, they decided to stop being a couple of idiots and just be a couple. Mr and Mrs Gasper invited them to Disneyland. They were touched, but declined the offer, mentioning that they would prefer to take a little tour of Normandy in the Lancia instead. 'Maybe bring back a case of bubbly, eh?' said Stefan with a wink for the Unvisibles. All this was fine by Nicky who *definitely* gave up doing the three-thing.

It might just be worth mentioning that after the jumping up and down and 'We're RICH!' business, Nicky and Oliver had a sit down in front of *The Bathers* on one of the padded seats they supply at the National Gallery for people who want to take a long, slow look. For quite a time they didn't say anything. They were just trying to take it all in, letting their minds and their eyes wander, trying to connect the crazy colourful dots that made up the extraordinary events of the past few days.

Oliver was immersed in this new experience – of enjoying just sitting quietly with his friend – and with the prospect of so many things turning out nicely, maybe even school. Then he suddenly became aware of a figure in the painting standing in the water. Not the kid with the sun hat who was calling through his cupped hands. No, there was another kid in the water behind him – a pale, indistinct kid, quite tall, with his back to everybody. 'That's you, that is,' he laughed, pointing him out and giving Nicky a nudge in the ribs. 'The kid that hates being noticed.'

'Well if you ask me, he looks more like you!' grinned Nicky. 'Look at the colour of his hair!' It was exactly the same red.

'Hard to believe, en it?' said Oliver. 'Us two. The Unvisibles.'

'It is,' said Nicky. 'You don't think we . . . kind of made it up, do you?'

'I know what you mean. But if it didn't happen, it's weird that we both think it did. Know what I mean?'

'Would you do it again? Go invisible?'

'Maybe. What about you? Hey!'

'What's the matter?'

Oliver jumped up and thrust his hands into his pockets. 'I've lost that bit of paper with the words on! Did I give it back to you?'

Nicky had a rummage in his own pockets. 'You may have done. Maybe I left it in my other trousers. Don't worry; it doesn't matter for now, does it? It'll turn up some time. Bound to.'

'Unbelievable!' said Oliver, shaking his head and looking at his dad's sketches one more time before wrapping them carefully in the jumper his sister had made him bring and tucking them safely into his rucksack. 'The whole thing – it's fantastic.'

That was when they heard the sound of a mobile ringing the theme from *Star Wars* somewhere very close by. Oliver started patting all his pockets, looking for his phone – but there was nothing there.

'Oh, I forgot I still had this!' said Nicky, and reached into his pocket. His hand came out empty, too.

'What?' asked Oliver.

Before Nicky could answer, his palm began to play the theme music from *Star Wars*. He lifted it gingerly to his ear, feeling for the 'answer' button. 'H-hello?'

'Nicky?' came Stefan Dudzinski's voice. Nicky held the invisible mobile so that Oliver could hear as well. 'We're just on our way round now from the National Portrait Gallery. We've had a *great* time. But listen, your mum tells me you don't have a mobile. So how come I've got your number on mine – and how come you're answering it?'

'Um,' said Nicky. He looked at Oliver who made a face and shrugged his shoulders, so he said the first thing that came into his head after 'Um'.

'*Chhoo muntar jaldi.*'

GAYLORD RG